Running the Sheets

Running the Sheets

To the REAL "Jenna at Staples". Thanks for your help with this book. Enjoy the stories!

Jim T.

James Tallon

Copyright © 2012 by James Tallon.

Library of Congress Control Number: 2012914798
ISBN: Hardcover   978-1-4797-0067-7
              Softcover   978-1-4797-0066-0
              Ebook   978-1-4797-0068-4

All rights reserved. No part of this book may be reproduced or transmitted in any form or by any means, electronic or mechanical, including photocopying, recording, or by any information storage and retrieval system, without permission in writing from the copyright owner.

This book was printed in the United States of America.

Rev. date: 04/09/2013

To order additional copies of this book, contact:
Xlibris Corporation
1-888-795-4274
www.Xlibris.com
Orders@Xlibris.com
120752

Contents

Running the Sheets 11
The Town 13
Exodus 16
The Babysitters 20
The Lodge 27
Public Enemy No. 1 30
Humiliation 34
Entrepreneurialism 38
Big Turk 42
Country Squire 51
Never Cry Wolf 57
Das Boot 64
Crazy Greg 70
The Witches' House 77
Harry and the Go-Cart 84
The Parade 96
That Smell 105
Here's Johnny! 114
The Russian and the Dwarf 120
Das Boot—Part II 125
The Skylight 134
Tuesdays with Mom 138
Mary 146
Burning the Leaves 152
Appendices 156
Acknowledgments 161

For Harper and Patrick

And for J.T.

I think it was hockey player, lawyer, writer, politician Ken Dryden who once wrote that we all have a nostalgia for that magical time in our childhoods when everything seemed perfect—a golden age that combines memory and incident in such a way to transcend actual experience. Looking back on my childhood at The Poplars, I can't imagine a more idyllic introduction to the nuances of life than those ten memorable summers I spent with my family, friends and countless visitors at that extraordinary place on the shores of Newboro Lake.

Running the Sheets

My favourite pastime in the summer was something my brother and I discovered by accident while playing a game of hide and seek with a couple friends. By noon, housekeeping staff had cleaned the guestrooms and hauled the linens and towels to the laundry room. The sheets were cleaned on site; the towels sent out. The washing machines were the antiquated wringer variety that literally squeezed the dirt out of the linens. The process was time consuming. There were no dryers in the laundry room that I can remember, certainly none large enough to accommodate that many sheets. Marge Pritchard, the laundry woman, pinned the freshly washed sheets to clotheslines that traversed the lawn just outside the laundry room.

There were five rows of clotheslines. At busy times, all the lines were draped with newly laundered sheets. The sheets would hang in such a way that a kid could run through all five rows and back again without losing contact with them. When more kids joined in, the odds of a collision increased, although I don't recall this ever happening. I do remember the soothing softness of the drying sheets and the soapy smell of detergent as we manoeuvred through the maze in the balmy summer air.

The game would go on for a while before Marge would storm out of the laundry room and chase us away. Marge was also the woman who reported to my father that Paul, Steven Moore and I had been playing with matches in the laundry room one summer afternoon, which led to a stern reprimand. My father may have even threatened a spanking. This was one of the rare times my father was angry with both of us at the same time. Usually it was one, not the other. Often it was Paul, not me. Not that I was any more innocent, but I think I was cleverer about hiding my mischief.

We were kids. The clean white sheets and our dirty hands were not an ideal combination. But we could not leave them untouched. We would return the next day and the next to run the sheets, despite the repeated warnings of Marge, the not so beautiful laundrette.

The Town

You've driven through this town many times. You know the kind. If there weren't a reduced speed limit warning sign, you wouldn't notice it at all.

At slower speeds the town seems larger and possesses the usual small town qualities. Old wood frame houses, post office, general store, town hall, narrow side streets and perhaps even a gas station or a restaurant. Outwardly the town offers very little other than an eerie sense of sameness.

Because these towns are everywhere you forget them by the time you reach the *thank you for visiting* sign on the outskirts.

Each of these towns has stories, characters, and traditions, and each has thrived and faltered throughout its history. Yet these towns continue to exist and offer a life and memories to current and former inhabitants.

This is an account of a decade spent in such a place, specifically a snapshot of life at a fishing lodge in Newboro, a small town on the Rideau System in rural Eastern Ontario. The story is not so much about the town as it is about the people who inhabited it and the collective experiences of these characters.

* * *

There is a long, meandering highway that enters the town from the east. On the fringes there are farm houses for small working farms that have seen better days. The barns and silos stand out in particular.

From a distance the scene is ominous. The barns appear dilapidated and ready to collapse, the silos elusive. On closer inspection there is evidence of activity: a stack of hay, a block of salt, a watering trough, some fencing, a closed gate, a tractor, some feed bags, and a few grazing dairy cows.

One year, five years, ten years: the image doesn't change. Working family farms—a concept from another time—still linger today refusing to die out completely. These are the images that dominate the landscape on either side of the town.

* * *

The town of Newboro owes its existence to the construction of the Rideau Canal in the mid-1830s. The town developed out of necessity: The Royal Miners and Sappers (an engineer soldier) who built the canal needed permanent shelter and constructed log homes near the canal site. Merchants set up shop to meet the needs of those working on the canal. The town's population in 1850 was 300 people. Despite being devastated by fires, including the "Kennedy Fire" that destroyed 17 buildings in one day in 1874, Newboro recovered and was officially incorporated as a village in 1876.

The B & W Railway used to run through the town, and it was an important part of the town's identity in the early 1900s. The railway closed in 1953, another victim of the Ontario highway projects of the 1950s.[1]

Today, the population of Newboro is 310, give or take a couple families. Remove electricity and asphalt and a few other modern amenities and the town looks very much like it did 150 years ago. The canal is still there and the locks, now electric, are an integral part of the Rideau Canal system. It is also host to one of four blockhouses built by Colonel John By to protect the Rideau from attack by the Americans. Royal Miners and

---

[1] http://www.rideau-info.com/canal/driving/map-newboro.html

Sappers, victims of malaria, are the primary inhabitants of the Anglican cemetery that overlooks the canal just west of town.

The primary industry in Newboro is tourism, specifically fishing which has been the main attraction for close to 100 years. The American invasion is welcomed.

Exodus

My family in 1968 consisted of my mother and father, my sister Cathy, my brother Paul, our cocker spaniel Skipper, and me. We lived in the middle class Montreal suburb of Dollard des Ormeau, which was inhabited primarily by Anglophones in the 1960s. My dad worked for Bell Canada, my mom was a nurse but was home with my brother and me. My sister was school age.

I will provide some physical description of Paul and me here to quell some of the rumours. Paul has dark hair, blue eyes and a darker complexion, just like my father; I have fairer skin, strawberry blonde hair and, back then, freckles splattered across my nose. The contrast between the two of us couldn't have been greater, especially since my mother was a brunette with a darker complexion.

The running joke was I got my red hair from the milkman in Montreal. He did have a similar hair colour to mine, my mother was home alone all day, and it was the swingin' 60s.

While I often repeated this story when asked to explain where I got my red hair, I never understood the moral implications of what I was saying. Later, this proved disastrous when my dad, in a fit of spiritual urgency, decided to invite three nuns from St. Edward's Church in Westport to our home for dinner in the winter of 1973, and the subject of my hair colour came up. During dessert, I explained to the nuns what I knew to be the truth of my heritage. They sat stone faced and silent as I recounted the popular theory of my conception.

My mother excused herself from the table, my father cleared his throat and my sister stifled a giggle. At the conclusion of my story, awkward silence lingered as the guests dutifully finished their apple crisp. After the three sisters departed, my father informed me that some stories were intended for a family audience only, and they were not to be shared with devoted followers of the Lord. I was still not clear on my real father's identity, however.

Paul was two in 1968, Cathy was seven and I was three. From the outside our life looked comfortable, and from what I have heard and what very few memories I have of the 1960s, it probably was.

If you want comfort, predictability and security, the suburbs used to provide this for most young families in cities all over North America.

For a child of three it's impossible to perceive much of anything. The nuances of human behaviour and emotion thankfully elude a toddler. Experience and memory are disjointed and scattered. I know I had a mother and father, but I have no recollection of the mood of the household.

The family snapshots from the time show a family doing typical family things. Christmas mornings, birthday parties, baptisms, family trips, days at the beach. Everyone appears content.

Dad, Jimmy, Cathy and Paul, Hollywood Beach, Fla. 1968

I have a photo of my smiling father and two of his Bell Canada cronies dressed in standard issue *Mad Men* business suits and narrow ties fawning over a voluptuous Playboy bunny at the now defunct Playboy Club in Montreal. He does not look unhappy in this photo.

My father (next to bunny) at Playboy Club in Montreal

I suppose everything was fine. But dissatisfaction and yearning are difficult for a child to detect. Dreams and desires can weigh heavily on an individual who is stuck in a place he doesn't want to be.

Historical revisionists would claim that most Anglophones in Quebec in the late 1960s were a tad uneasy. Bombs in postal boxes and threats of kidnappings tend to do that to people. These external influences pale in comparison to something else that affects individuals: a restlessness of spirit. Terrorists and separatists come and go. Internal longings stick around, and one can't ignore them forever.

It is with this desire for change that my father decided to pack up his suburban family and their predictable existence and venture into the unknown world of rural living. Not the *let's get away from it all* rural living, but rather the *let's get away from it all and enter a life about which we know absolutely nothing* living, where the characters we encountered would be no less eccentric than the characters one would find on the Metro in Montreal on any Friday night.

My dad's idea of escape was to purchase a fishing lodge in a pint-sized outpost in Eastern Ontario, without training, experience, or any idea of what to expect. Saying he—I think my mom was along for the ride—walked into it blindly would be an understatement. But if we all knew the outcomes of our endeavours we probably wouldn't undertake half the adventures we do. I thank my dad for his decision—impulsive as it may have been—to abandon city life and head to the country.

The Babysitters

In the winter of 1968, the five of us and our cocker spaniel migrated to Newboro, Ontario. With my mother preoccupied with three young children, my father had to get ready for opening, which was scheduled for early May to coincide with the official beginning of pike and walleye seasons.

The former owners' offer to help out if necessary eased the transition to some extent, but they were elderly and provided nostalgic wisdom and little else. My parents elected to keep Louie Moore on as handyman and waterfront mystic. This proved to be the best decision my parents ever made at the lodge. Louie's calm demeanour and his expert knowledge of The Poplars' complex infrastructure, specifically septic tanks and water filtration systems, made him my father's go-to guy, especially in times of crisis. Louie was Tonto, my dad the Lone Ranger.

For the first two seasons, May through Thanksgiving, my parents struggled, learning mostly from their missteps and getting by on humour and the grace of God more than anything else. My dad's Bell Canada mandated Dale Carnegie training proved more useful than ever. Doing his best Willy Loman impersonation, he liked to remind us all that personality mattered, especially in the resort business.

My parents persevered, becoming more comfortable with each new season at the lodge; however, they were rarely available for quality family time in the summer. They saw this as neglect, which it was not, but we couldn't tell them this.

I have few memories of those early summer seasons at The Poplars other than of the odd birthday party, fireworks display, outdoor meal and the babysitters my parents hired every summer to keep my brother and me from drowning.

Jimmy and Paul, summer 1969

The babysitters were generally exquisite. They were teenage girls who looked and smelled delightful. My dad may have had more of a say in their hiring than I realized, and perhaps he had the seductive Playboy bunnies in mind when he made his staffing choices. I know if I were in charge of hiring I would have used these lovely specimens as my templates.

By the summer of 1969 my brother and I were in the care of these sitters most of the time, and while I was too young to develop vivid fantasies I was able to develop "feelings" for these teenage girls. These feelings were simple I suppose and consisted of a combination of euphoric excitement and mild contentment whenever I was around them.

I thought it possible for them to develop feelings for me, a pre-pubescent freckle-faced kid. I am not sure how my brother felt about the sitters. He was one year younger and much less aware of the opposite sex than I. He seemed to be more interested in fishing, frogs, hamsters and snakes. I, on the other hand, was a lady's man and did not lack confidence around these young women.

Shelley Clemenhagen was my favourite. She was a goddess in my eyes.

Shelley was tall, slim, with long brown hair and sleepy brown eyes, just the way I like my goddesses. I remember her long eyelashes in particular. She usually wore jeans and a t-shirt. She lived on her family's farm just outside Newboro. She would often take us to her farm where we would get to see various livestock and multitudes of barn cats and kittens. There were always too many to count. But kittens didn't matter to me; it was time with Shelley that did. She was enchanting.

There is a black and white photograph of my sister and me holding some kittens. I am sitting on Shelley's backside as she lies on the porch in front of her house. I must have been about five, and I look as content as a five-year-old can look. And I think this photograph captures the essence of my relationship with Shelley. We just knew we were meant to be together. I mean I knew this. For her it was just a summer job and an opportunity to escape farm work. But I would like to think that she was at least aware of my love for her.

Shelley, Cathy, three barn cats and me

Other babysitters came and went and an honourable mention goes to Barbara Fleming who was also a seductive temptress in a cerebral sort of way. She seemed to favour my brother, so my memories of her are not as romantic. I do recall her once pulling my brother from the lake after he had tripped on the dock inside a boathouse. The memory is vivid, as the tumble seemed to happen in slow motion.

My brother and I were always falling into the lake, but this tumble was unusual for two reasons: First, it was an indoor fall (we usually fell in the lake in the wide open day time for all to see) and, second, it happened at a time of day when the sun was just starting to set and the angle of the sun's rays sneaking in under the crooked boathouse illuminated the water in the boathouse. The water should have been dark and murky, but it was a shimmering amber. My brother fell into this glowing pool somehow adjusting in mid air to land backwards in the water, arms and legs splayed.

It is probably the first vivid image I recall from those early years at the lodge, and the moment belongs to my brother being rescued by the brainy sun queen. I am not sure if he remembers this the way I do, but it solidified his relationship with Barbara Fleming.

The only other babysitter I recall, and I will not use her real name, was the one my mother fired thanks to my sister Cathy. I will call her Stella . . . no wait . . . I will call her Helga. Sorry, Germany, nothing personal.

My dad must not have been involved in the hiring process for this one because the sitter who followed these two temptresses was no award winner. She was plain mean. And she hated kids, especially kids with strawberry blonde hair and freckles. She was ugly too, and she never smiled and . . . she was our babysitter in 1972 when I was seven and my brother was six.

Her goal was simple: prevent us from having any fun. If our activity was enjoyable, she would put a stop to it. She used to look at her watch all the time eagerly anticipating the day's end. Friends would come to visit, and Helga would send them home because they did something wrong according to her book of unwritten rules.

Jamie Forbes, who was a year older than I and the son of Ruth the cook at the lodge, came over once, and we emptied our plastic kids' pool on the lawn in front of our house.

Driven by our mutual desire for fame, Jamie and I decided to flip the pool over, put it on our heads and run blindly around the front lawn until we crashed into something—trees, swing set, my brother, the house, the babysitter. According to our ever-attentive, evil babysitter, this was an unsafe activity, and we could be injured.

Helga: "I have taken a babysitting course. This conduct was not covered in either the course or the manual!"
Jamie: "Aaagh . . . Oeewww."
Helga: "I demand that the two of you cease this inappropriate behaviour immediately!"
Me: "Grrrrr . . ."
Helga: "If the two of you do not stop this instant, I will have no choice but to inform your parents of your childish behaviour, not to mention your careless disregard for my feelings and authority."
Jamie: "Huh?"

The chase lasted five minutes before Helga lassoed Jamie, reprimanded him again and sent him straight home. As he walked down the road toward his house, Helga continued to heckle him.

"I know your mother, and I am sure she will be very displeased with your behaviour today. You have not seen nor heard the end of me, young man!" she yelled.

Following this incident was a tense dinner with the babysitter, my sister, my brother and me. I refused to accept her explanation, which wasn't really an explanation at all; it was more of a dismissive demand to comply with her wishes which she based solely on fear.

On the menu that fateful night was the obligatory Friday night meatloaf prepared by my mother but *placed in the oven* by Helga. All she had to do was cook it for an hour or for however long meatloaf should be cooked, but she couldn't do it because she was too busy administering her totalitarian justice.

Helga: "After what you put me through this afternoon, Jimmy, the least you could do is comply with my wishes and the wishes of your mother and eat your dinner as you are expected."
Me: "I can't eat this."
Helga: "Why not? It's a perfectly delectable meal that I worked very hard preparing."

Me: "No you didn't. My mother made it. You just put it in the oven."
Cathy: "I put it in the oven."
Helga: "Cathy, you were not asked to participate in this exchange. I cooked the meal and you will consume every last morsel before you leave this table."
Me: "There isn't enough ketchup in the world to make me eat this."

The meatloaf was slightly overcooked (her words) or burnt (my words). It was so charred that I refused to eat it. I put a fork full in my mouth, but I couldn't chew it, let alone swallow it. I began my protest, spitting out the meatloaf and refusing to eat any more.

Helga had had enough. She grabbed me by the arm and pulled me from the table. She proceeded to spank me in a cold and deliberate manner. Was this spanking a key component of the totalitarian babysitting course she had taken in Stuttgart? If Barbara or Shelley were delivering this spanking, I don't think I would have minded at all . . . but this was Helga. She hated me. I hated her. The harder she hit me the more meatloaf I sprayed in her direction. Overcome by pain and humiliation, I burst into tears.

Helga didn't stop. My tears inspired her to strike me harder.

Meanwhile, my sister and brother were watching from the table. At the time, I assumed they were enjoying the show. But without uttering a word, my sister rose from the table, tip-toed down the basement stairs, walked out the back door of the house and sprinted to the lodge where it was dinner time for all the guests.

This was a hectic time in the dining room and the kitchen, especially for my mom. My dad used to disappear at critical moments during the day, usually to go golfing, so my mom had to shoulder the majority of the responsibilities. This consisted of supervising unpredictable help, from melancholy dishwashers to erratic waitresses and cooks. Often there would be a staffing crisis of some sort, usually by the time my dad was on the fourth or fifth hole at the local golf course.

My sister found my mom in the lodge kitchen and informed her of the dispute between Helga and me. I would like to think that my mom dropped everything to storm up the hill to the house and confront Helga in front of us kids. Maybe this was how it played out.

But I think my mother handled this matter as she did most issues: in a tactful and firm manner. My mom fired Helga that day, and I have my sister Cathy to thank for it.

From then on, our parents gave my brother, Cathy and me more freedom around the lodge. We no longer required supervision every waking hour. Cathy became our new sitter by default that summer, but we adored her and would do anything she asked of us.

This was a turning point for our summers. Paul and I now had the opportunity to go about our lives untethered. Our only instructions were to not go too near the lake.

The Lodge

The Poplars Resort opened for business in the 1940s, transformed from a private family retreat to a commercial facility to capitalize on the surplus income and vacation needs of the post-war era. Its primary function was to cater to American outdoorsmen and their families seeking reliable fishing and a relaxing summer escape in a northern climate. This has remained the main focus of The Poplars to present day. It thrives on the myth of the big one that got away.

The fishing resort sits on a gently sloping hill with wood frame guest houses scattered around the perimeter. Numerous overgrown poplar trees and their brittle branches tower over the property. This is how the resort looked in 1968 and, minus a few poplar trees, is how it looks today. "Rustic" is one word to describe the atmosphere.

In the 1970s, The Poplars' capacity was approximately 70 guests during peak season and is still the same today. The main lodge, dining room and waterfront are the principal areas of activity. All buildings on the property are painted white with bright turquoise trim. There used to be a beautiful arched wooden bridge, recognizable at a considerable distance on the water, connecting docks on the waterfront, but the wood rotted. Sometime in the mid 1980s, The Poplars' brain trust decided to dismantle the bridge and to not replace it.

The Poplars with arched bridge, circa 1975 (postcard)

The centrepiece of the property was the main lodge. Constructed in the 1920s well before the guest houses and other buildings, the over-sized cottage was a family vacation retreat for Stephen K. Bresee, who owned a Chevrolet dealership in Syracuse, New York. In the 1920s the property, known as Villa Dale, consisted of the main lodge and boathouse. Mr. Bresee died in 1936, and his family sold the property after his death. Villa Dale became a commercial property in the 1940s, and the new owners, Art and Ruby Simmons, changed its name to The Poplars.

The main lodge's design and contents reflected the time period in which it was built. The colonial revival style, popular at the time all over North America in the 1920s, is the dominant design element for the main lodge. Outside, the design is simple, the façade symmetrical with banks of larger windows running the length of the front and sides of the structure, each offering a unique view of the lake. At the side of the building, which also serves as the main entrance to the lodge, there is a full length screened-in porch offering views in three directions.

The first floor of the lodge is larger than the second floor allowing for unique design elements for the upper level, which rested on the lower level with gently slanting roof sections covering the upstairs guest rooms and bathrooms. The centrepieces of the building were an over-sized stone fireplace that took up most of the east interior wall of the main sitting area and the large peaked skylight of dense green antique glass in the ceiling of the dining room.

In the front porch area were two swinging couches that in the spring held on to the musty smell of winter a little longer than the rest of the building. There was also a floor model Coca Cola machine, the one with the top that lifted up to reveal a maze of channels for the bottle to travel before the customer yanked it out. Soft drinks sold for 25 cents at the lodge unless one knew the owner or possessed stealthy, skinny arms.

On the lake side of the porch was a bumper pool table, with its strange rubber knobs in various strategic locations on the table. This bastardized variation on the traditional game of pool was an anomaly in a place of tradition and simplicity.

The room next to the bumper pool table served two purposes: First, it was the overflow room when the dining room was full, and more importantly it was the games room containing a pinball machine, with a Las Vegas theme, a floor model Pong video game and some card tables. In the summer months, nightly card games of bridge, poker and euchre would be commonplace at these tables. With plenty of practice, Paul and I became the pinball wizards of the lodge, vying for the crown of champion with ever-increasing high scores.

The main lodge produced a variety of olfactory delights depending on the time of year. In spring it was the cool and musty dampness of the place when it was first opened in late April. Boards down from the screened-in porch area and windows open for the first time in months ushered out the mustiness. Upstairs the scent of moth balls predominated as the guest rooms aired out as well.

By early May and opening, the traditional mid-summer smells of the lodge returned. The hardwood floors, cherry wood ceilings and walls, the dark red leather couches and the roaring fire combined to create a familiar and welcoming aroma. I recall as well detecting a sweetness to the smell of the main lodge and was never certain if this was due to the aromas emanating from the kitchen or more likely because of the big gold-fish bowl of *Double Bubble* bubble gum and the variety of flavours of old-fashioned stick candies available in the gift shop.

Public Enemy No. 1

With increased freedom, my brother and I had greater access to the community of Newboro. Friends we had at school and saw infrequently when we were with our babysitters became important parts of our lives.

Dougie McViety was the funniest kid we knew. He was a few years older than Paul and I. He had this interesting way of talking and storytelling. He was full of expressions and language we had never heard before. When he told stories, he told them in his unusual nasal voice. We were never sure if this was for effect or not.

But it wasn't his voice that was funny. It was Dougie. Pick a swear word and Dougie would know how to use it as a verb, noun, adverb, adjective and even pronoun. This colourful language flowed off his tongue. He even instructed Paul and me on the power of inflection and emphasis when swearing. We were set for life. He was a bona fide profanity grammarian, not uncommon in those parts at that time.

There was another quality about Dougie that I should mention, so you will understand why my father banned Dougie from the lodge.

Dougie had a flat face. Yes, a flat face from his forehead down to his chin. His nose was especially flat. I understand now that this can be attributed to genetics, but at the time I had no idea why Dougie's face was flat. Who was I to judge? I had—still have—a large head, too big for my body.

Those "one-size-fits-all" hats do not come as advertised, at least not for everyone. Let the litigation begin.

The rumour going around town was that when Dougie was younger his mother got so angry with him that she hit him square in the face with a frying pan. For Paul and me this explanation made sense, as domestic frying pan incidents were in the news throughout the early 1970s.

In the summer of 1975, Paul, Dougie and I could do almost anything. We drank gallons of Coke, which we would steal from the floor model soft drink machine in the main lodge. It wasn't really stealing, however, because our parents would give us the 25 cents daily just for staying out of the lake. Thanks to Dougie's crazy anecdotes the Coke often ended up shooting out of our noses during convulsive fits of laughter.

We played pinball and pool daily, either in the small games room at the lodge or at Vic's store "up street" as Dougie called it. We would roam all over the town with Dougie. I don't think Dougie had his own bike or he had to share it with his brothers or something, so we walked everywhere.

Dougie was a gifted architect as well. With Dougie, we built the best forts using real wood, windows and shingles we found around the lodge property. We painted our clubhouses with leftover paint we borrowed from the pump house. Dougie was a master with a hammer and nails. Paul and I would get the materials, and Dougie would put the stuff together, all without a blueprint. We even had a picture window in one of our forts thanks to Dougie. Not everything was plumb, but it was close.

Dougie introduced us to culture, too. He had a Simon and Garfunkel record, the soundtrack to *The Graduate*, and we listened to it often in our living room. Dougie knew all the lyrics by heart, and he did an especially fine job with *Scarborough Fair*. This is the first memory I have of music in my life other than the easy-listening eight track tapes we endured when driving with my parents. By the age of six I knew the words to *Moon River* by heart. Dougie introduced us to a new world of music, and we wanted to hear more. But he only had the one album. And this album didn't even belong to him. Dougie was adept at borrowing stuff, not so skilled at returning it.

Dougie considered the game of cowboys and Indians outdated. He said cops and robbers was more entertaining and more violent because both sides had guns. As a result, the quality of our arsenal improved as he seemed to have an unlimited supply of caps for our cap guns.

He informed us that when robbers rob banks, they use disguises to hide their identities. He asked us to steal some pantyhose from our mother's dresser. It seemed like an odd request at the time, but Paul and I complied and produced one pair of pantyhose for Dougie.

He declared it was time for a more realistic game of cops and robbers. He said he would play the role of bank robber, and Paul and I would be the cops.

Dougie: "It's time to grow up, boys. No one plays cowboys and Indians anymore."
Paul: "But we've always played cowboys and Indians."
Dougie: "Enough is enough, God damn-it! Let's play a real game, one that men play."
Me: "Men *play* cops and robbers? I haven't seen any adults *playing* cops and robbers. Men rob banks for real. Should we do that?"
Dougie: "No, of course not! But if you have any intention of ever becoming a man you might want to upgrade the quality of games you play."

He told us to wait outside.

Standing in the parking lot behind our house and adjacent to the lodge, Paul and I waited for Dougie to emerge from our basement door. We didn't have to wait long, but the anticipation was killing us. Finally, he burst through the back door, a stocking pulled over his head and guns blazing.

Paul and I were frightened. We were the cops. But we froze. The scene was too realistic. His method acting lessons in Westport had paid off. He wasn't Dougie anymore; he was John Dillinger or Baby Face Nelson . . . make that Flat Face McViety. Plus, he was wearing our mother's pantyhose on his head. He ran by us swearing and firing his cap guns in all directions.

"You *&$#in' coppers. You can't stop me!" he yelled as he raced by us. He tore down the hill to the lawn in front of the main lodge.

Our stupors didn't last long. We were the good guys. We had a job to do. There was no time for fear or hesitation. Knowing that justice was on our side, we chased this nylon-clad menace to society down the hill.

It was then I heard the high-pitched and terrified shriek of a woman . . . or it could have been a pre-pubescent boy. I wasn't certain.

We arrived on the scene seconds later, our cap guns firing. We discovered a distraught elderly guest from Brooklyn. Her husband held her close, her face buried in his chest. She was shaking and sobbing. Dougie was lingering off to the side, the pantyhose still on his head.

My father was standing in the middle of this grouping. Numerous guests were mulling about. Everyone was staring at Dougie. My dad was likely wishing he was on the golf course somewhere or any place other than the front lawn of the lodge.

He glared at Paul and me. He glared at Dougie.

Dougie didn't look frightened at all. I don't think he understood what all the fuss was about. He was a terrifying sight. The pantyhose and his unusual face made a sinister combination, especially for an elderly woman from Brooklyn on vacation at The Poplars.

After apologizing to the guests, my dad took Dougie aside. They spoke briefly . . . very briefly. Paul and I were not included in their conversation.

My father sent Dougie McViety home that afternoon and decreed that Dougie was banned from the lodge indefinitely. Our punishment was light: We were allowed to play with Dougie, just not on the lodge property. My father ordered us to stay out of our mother's underwear drawer, too.

Humiliation

As the lengthy school year came to an end, the excitement for the two months of freedom that lay ahead was impossible for us to contain. We were smug in the knowledge that as our liberty increased with each passing year so too did the quality of our adventures.

The planning for the summer began early, often commencing the first week of June. We produced secret documents containing complex maps and diagrams, lists of names and places, and various disguise options. We hid this information in an old cigar box under my bed. Our plans relied heavily on the pursuits of the previous summer, for we now knew the limits and pitfalls of many of our more misguided endeavours. Annual updates were a necessity to ensure another satisfying summer.

However, there was some anxiety as the end of the school year approached as well.

Paul and I dreaded the traditional introduction to summer our father imposed on us: the skin-searing bean shave he facilitated the day following the last day of school.

Our parents displayed little concern for our hair during the winter and spring months. All we had to do was keep it clean and have the occasional trim.

School pictures from the time show Paul and me with longer, often unruly hair. Parental concern for their children's warmth during the cold winter months may have had something to do with this, or the fashion of the day may have played a role. David Cassidy, Leif Garrett, Adam Rich . . . even the Brady Bunch boys had long hair. But theirs was long year-round; ours was not.

It was the 1970s. While the waist length hair of the sixties was passé, the shoulder length unkempt mop style of the 70s had only just begun. And eye-brow grazing bangs were the craze of the day. If only Paul and I had been able to grow thick hedge-like sideburns, we would have been in 70's polyester heaven. Bushy moustaches would have been a nice touch too for obvious reasons: Chicks dug the facial hair back then. Thank you very much Mark Spitz and Burt Reynolds. You too, John Holmes.

Every summer my father decreed that short hair, skull white short, was in order. No matter how much we protested, my father's edict always carried the day. As he reminded us annually, he went through this as a kid, so we would too. Never too early to begin turning boys into marines, he would bugle.

He would have to drag us kicking and screaming to the station wagon for the short trip to Westport and Gary Murphy's Barbershop. It was always a sombre journey with minimal conversation. I detected a hint of sadistic pleasure from my dad as this may have been the one time of the year when he could put the screws to Jimmy and Paul for all their mischief from the previous summer. Rather than blow up at us when we screwed up, he just stored it away and had a cathartic release every June at the barbershop as Paul and I sat teary eyed, strapped into Sweeney Todd's chair.

The drive from Newboro to Westport was five minutes and thirty-eight seconds, assuming that one complied with the speed limit. But the humiliation trip seemed to take half that. I think my father drove faster than usual on this special day, the gleam of revenge in his eyes.

At the barbershop the atmosphere was funereal and jovial at the same time. Gary Murphy, the barber, was a heavy set man with a deep voice and perpetual smile on his face. He was a talker and the conversation in the shop was non-stop as soon as my dad and his two victims walked through the door.

On the wall of the shop were pictures of each available haircut option. The choices were numbered one to ten. Our cut was the number two, which may have had something to do with the type of blade Mr. Murphy used on the trimming shears. The "number two"! Despite our predicament, Paul and I were able to find humour in this.

Perhaps it should have been called *The Humiliation*.

It took no time at all. First Paul and then me, or first me and then Paul, it didn't really matter . . . our fates were sealed from the moments we were conceived. Six or seven pass-overs of the scalp with the shears and that was it—we were now bald young men with no chance whatsoever of getting a date for the first part of summer.

There's a Jim Carroll song from the late 70s entitled "People Who Died". Its lyrics are disturbing, but applicable in this instance: *Bobby got leukemia fourteen years old, looked like sixty-five when he died* . . . For my brother and me, it was THAT bad.

We couldn't look in the mirror, we couldn't look at each other, we couldn't say "Thank you, Mr. Murphy" even when our father prompted us. We were too traumatized to speak, let alone thank someone for butchering us.

My dad's insincere compliments would commence the moment Gary was finished with our heads.

"Now, you boys look like real men."
"That's a haircut—just like marines!"
"Doesn't it feel so much better to have all that hair buzzed off?"
"That's the style I had when I was your age, and I didn't mind."

We were thinking, *Please! Cut out the cheerleading act. Your job as our father is to foster self-esteem not destroy it.* It was worse than some of the hazing rituals on many university campuses in America. We were mortified.

Our ears were now completely visible as were our foreheads and the backs of our necks. Our heads were now nothing more than gritty sandpaper orbs. We were spectacles, and we had to go back to the lodge and face our friends and all the guests too. My sister was unable to contain her laughter for more than five seconds.

Years later examining some photographs our mother took after one of our agonizing barbershop ordeals, my brother quipped that we, especially me, looked like products of incest. That hurt. But it was true. The banjo playing mountain boy in the film *Deliverance* had nothing on us. And he could play a musical instrument, so at least he was amusing to some degree.

For days, we were in hiding; doing everything we could to avoid human contact. This was no easy task in the summer at The Poplars. Eventually, Paul and I donned a couple over-sized fishing caps and emerged from the shadows.

Entrepreneurialism

In late July of another year, in a desperate attempt to make money so we could attend the Delta Fair, Steven Moore, Paul and I devised a plan to increase our revenue. As it turned out, the scheme we came up with was ill-advised.

We decided the best way to make some quick cash was to establish a lawn-cutting business. We had one week before the fair and figured at worst if we cut five or six lawns at an inflated price we would have enough money for a day at the fair. Plus there were three of us, so we could share the labour.

There were some serious flaws with this plan. First of all, none of us was allowed to operate a power lawnmower without supervision. None of us was old enough to operate a power mower *with* supervision either. The second flaw, a significant one, was that we didn't have a lawnmower. We asked my dad if we could use The Poplars' lawnmower, and I believe his exact words were, "No."

Our plan was doomed from the start.

Without a lawnmower and without permission from our parents, we decided to pursue our scheme anyway. Our first goal was to entice some unsuspecting customers. We figured that older and single residents of Newboro would be the ideal targets for our scam. So we spent a day going door to door soliciting customers for our brand new lawn cutting business. We received rejection after rejection from each house we visited. We were discouraged.

If we went to the fair without our own money, we would be under the control of our parents. This was never a good scenario at fairs, where the arbitrary executive decisions of adults were joy-killers.

Near the end of our futile search, Steven suggested we approach Hilda Day, an older woman who lived at the end of By Street in Newboro. Hilda was Steven's aunt, so chances were pretty good she would agree to let us butcher her lawn.

We knocked on the door. We knocked again, this time much louder. She finally opened the door, but she didn't seem too pleased to see us. She appeared bewildered.

Ignoring Paul and me, Hilda asked Steven, "Who the hell are you?"
Steven: "I am Steven Moore, Ethel's son."
Hilda: "Who?"
Steven: "Ethel. Your sister. You are my aunt."
Hilda: "I know who my sister is! Why are you pestering me?"
Steven: "We want to cut your lawn."
Hilda: "Oh, that's all. Go right ahead."
Steven: "But we want money for cutting your lawn."
Hilda: "I figured as much. You sure you're Ethel's boy?"

She had a lot of nephews, so maybe it was hard to keep track of them all.

Steven did all the talking. He explained how the lawn cutting contract would work and how great Hilda's lawn would look. Then he asked if she owned a lawnmower. She said she hadn't owned one in years. She informed us that her son would show up once every couple of weeks with his own lawnmower and cut her lawn. But he was busy, she explained to us, and she would rather not bother him with the chore.

Steven informed her that we had our own lawnmower, so that wouldn't be a problem.

Had our own lawnmower? This guy was smooth. What were we going to use? Scissors? Hilda said that we could come back the next day and cut her lawn. She agreed to pay us $5. It wasn't a fortune, but it was a start.

We needed a lawnmower and spent the remainder of the day searching for one. We retraced our steps of earlier in the day when we had attempted to recruit customers for our lawn cutting business. At house after house, we inquired about the availability of a lawnmower for loan. Our desperation was evident for all to see, and we didn't find one person willing to lend us a working lawnmower.

Finally, a sympathetic Newboroite offered us a rusty, old push lawnmower she hadn't used in years. The blades were dull and the wheels wobbly. The donor advised us to liberally apply oil to various parts to get the contraption moving. We jumped at the chance and reminded ourselves that there were three of us, so using a manual push mower wouldn't be an insurmountable problem.

The next morning we showed up at Hilda's with the lawnmower. We oiled the wheels and the blade mechanism, so they were in working order. But it was heavy and one of the wheels wobbled. Pushing it all the way to Hilda's house had tired us out. Worst of all, her lawn was much larger than we realized, going all the way back to the fence at the end of her property. This was going to take forever.

We started mowing Hilda Day's lawn. We had neither a plan nor experience cutting grass. Because there were three of us we attacked the lawn haphazardly, often cutting diagonally one way and then in a straight line the next pass by. Worse, her grass was longer than we had realized. The dull blades of the mower did more bending of the grass than cutting. We took more frequent breaks as we started to tire from pushing this heavy lawnmower in the relentless July heat.

We persevered, however, and "finished" the job three hours later. Three hours later! At $5 dollars an hour. You do the math. Don't forget to divide by three.

The lawn may not have looked cut but it looked . . . different. Maybe Hilda wouldn't notice. Maybe she wasn't a stickler anyway. Maybe she would cut her long-lost nephew some slack.

Together the three of us walked up to Hilda's side door to inform her that we were finished and to collect our money. We knocked, but Hilda didn't answer the door. It was someone else. It was her son. He came outside without saying a word. He surveyed the property examining every inch of our cutting job. He then turned to us and reached into his pocket and pulled out his wallet. He removed a five dollar bill. Shaking his head, he handed our wages to Steven saying, "Boys, don't you ever come round here again, you hear?"

Our lawn cutting business lasted all of one day and one lawn. Our dream of Delta Fair independence was dead.

Big Turk

Steven Moore was hit by a milk truck when he was five. People claimed he was never the same after the accident. Apparently, he swallowed his tongue in the ordeal, and emergency personnel had taken some time to retrieve it. As a result, he was left with a prematurely raspy voice and sounded much older than he was. I think the same people who came up with the explanation for Dougie's unique features were also responsible for this theory.

He was older than Paul and I but the youngest in a family of eight children. Steven had more freedom by age five than we did at twice his age. I don't think he had a curfew. He was definitely streetwise . . . not necessarily *street-proofed,* however.

Steven's favourite foods were Big Turk chocolate bars and Pepsi. He wasn't interested in sports. He never complained about anything, and he was always interested in doing something, whether an adventure or just hanging out. He talked non-stop and had a perpetual smile on his face. Because he was with us every day, the outrageous stuff he may or may not have done doesn't stand out with the exception of one stunt that attracted everyone's attention.

A white Grecian style statue, made from either granite or limestone, sat—and still sits—on the front lawn of the lodge in plain view of the main dining room. The statue is of a fully nude male figure, possibly the god Mercury, and is mounted on a cement pedestal.

Guests at the lodge used to joke that my father posed for the sta' when he had muscles. The figure itself is five feet high, the pedestal roughly three feet high. An obscure artist painstakingly sculpted the mythical figure and painted it white from head to toe and all parts in between.

Statue of Mercury

Though no one knew for sure why the statue was there, everyone considered it the finest statue for miles. My parents warned Paul and me not to touch it for fear of it toppling. We adhered to this rule, but no one ever said that we could not paint the statue, which is exactly what Steven Moore decided to do one afternoon when he was bored and no one was around.

He lifted a can of bright cherry red paint and a brush from the pump house and decided to provide the statue with a much-needed makeover.

For us kids the most fascinating part of the statue was the groin region because it was a statue of a male figure, but the genitalia didn't look like male genitalia. The scrotum was stretched up and over the penis so that the figure's genitals took on the appearance of a sea shell. This was most perplexing for Steven, Paul and me. Steven decided to bring attention to this anatomical inaccuracy.

He painted the genital anomaly a brilliant cherry red. The contrast between the bright red genitals and the white of the rest of the statue was striking. It didn't take long for the guests to notice. Word spread that an art hater had defaced the sacred statue. Eventually, someone informed my parents. When they saw the touched up statue, they were mortified but amused at the same time. I recall my dad cracking a slight smile.

The short investigation naturally pointed to Paul and me, since the groin region was in reach of both of us, and we did have access to paint. Moreover, even at a young age we were huge fans of Renaissance art and sculpture. What kid isn't?

Seeking the spotlight, it didn't take long for Steven to step forward and acknowledge his guilt. For him it must have been akin to attending his own funeral. He could only observe the commotion for so long before he had to say something.

Because his father, Louie, was the most important employee at the lodge, Steven's punishment was light. My parents didn't banish him from The Poplars. He wasn't sent home. Most important, they didn't inform his mother. All my dad asked him to do was to find some white paint and complete another touch-up job. The only catch was that he had to complete this task in front of a live audience of guests and staff in broad daylight. He did this with a smile on his face.

* * *

In summer months, most of our days started with a visit from Steven. Outside our bedroom window was a large TV antenna tower. Steven quickly discovered that the best method to get Paul and me out of bed in the morning was to scale this antenna and pound on the window until we responded. Interrupting the soothing din of rustling poplar trees in the morning, Steven's gravelly voice startled us every time.

Steven was a daily fixture in our lives, and his sense of adventure and curiosity was an inspiration for Paul and me. Steven knew Newboro and the surrounding area better than we did. He would take us places we had never been before, sometimes on bike, sometimes on foot. We knew a day with Steven would never be dull.

One place we frequented was an impressive chunk of glacial rock we called Spy Rock, located in the middle of Farmer Whalen's pasture next to the Rideau Canal; the other was the remains of the B&W railway bridge that used to span the canal.

The stone work for the railway bridge was still in place, but the bridge had long been demolished. A 100 foot drop off from either side was all that remained. There were no barriers at the edge of either abutment. This was the 1970s—safety wasn't a priority. Neither were lawsuits.

Even more surprising was that Steven was allowed near the canal at all. On a summer day in the late 1960s, one of Steven's older brothers was playing near the canal and fell in. He was by himself at the time and was not a strong swimmer. He drowned. Steven never spoke of this event, but for some reason he was always drawn to the lake and to the canal. We all were.

Early in life, one of Steven's older brothers gave him the nickname Hazel. The reason for this was not clear at the time and is still not clear to this day. Unfortunately for Steven, while some nicknames don't stick, others do. The name Hazel stuck, and from his early years he was no longer Steven. Everyone called him Hazel: at school, around town, adults, kids. Even visitors to Newboro knew Steven as Hazel.

Steven never complained. It was only his mother, Ethel, who took offence to the nickname. If we used this moniker around her, she'd remind us that her son's name was Steven.

So Paul and I made it a point to call Steven by his given name. With everyone else referring to him as Hazel, this was no easy task. Over time, we were able to resist this temptation to conform, and he was forever Steven to us.

At the old canal bridge abutment Steven, Paul and I used to sit on the ledge with our feet dangling over the edge. Looking back, this was a really stupid thing to do.

First of all, none of us was a very strong swimmer—not that that would have mattered much with the 100-foot free fall and the shallow canal below. Secondly, we were kids and we lacked coordination and judgement. The stone at the edge was loose and jagged and any of us with the slightest misstep could have gone over the edge. There would have been nothing anyone could have done to stop this from happening. But it didn't happen.

We sat sometimes for entire afternoons on the edge of the bridge waving at boaters, throwing rocks, eating candy, or just wasting our day. There was an unspoken rule of respect when we were there. No one would ever fool around and put another in danger. We watched out for each other and made sure that the other person was mindful of the dangers. Because of this, and I think also because of Steven's older brother, this forbidding place became one of the safest places we visited.

Spy Rock was a name the locals stole from the neighbouring community of Westport. In Westport, there was Foley Mountain, which had the real Spy Rock—an elevated rocky ledge that overlooks the village of Westport, surrounding farmland and the Upper Rideau Lake. The original Spy Rock was a popular hangout for tourists during the day and local teenagers at night.

In Newboro, our Spy Rock was not as popular but it was no less dramatic. Our Spy Rock was a behemoth of a boulder that rested in the middle of a farmer's field on the outskirts of town. Nearby was a line of hydro towers, and the cicada-like hum of the electricity passing through these power lines was ever-present when we visited the rock.

The boulder stood out impressively from the flatness of the field. It was high enough, probably 12 feet, and large and round enough to require some effort to climb, and it was generally accessible to any kid with some coordination. I am sure older teenagers visited the rock at other times, and we did find some charred kitchen knives there. But we felt it was ours during the day. We would go there daily. Sometimes with snacks for lunch or sometimes with cap guns, or sometimes just to hide out from the fictitious man-hunters we evaded daily.

Eventually, the thrill of getting to the rock replaced the excitement of conquering the rock. Because it was a farmer's field there were often cows grazing nearby. Among these cows, a different coloured cow, larger and more menacing, ambled through the grass. Whether it was a bull or not didn't matter, because we made up our minds very early that it was, and it was dangerous. We were convinced that at some point this bull would chase us, especially if we provoked it or if we wore red clothing.

We would park our bikes at the gate, calculate the distance between us, the rock and the "bull" and then make a run for it, assuming of course that the bull had nothing better to do than to chase kids all day. The slightest movement or acknowledgment from the bull would set us off and confirm our belief that we were living dangerously. We would sprint as fast as we could to the rock and safety. Climbing the boulder became more exciting when we convinced ourselves that it was a matter of life and death.

The thrill of this running with the bulls never dissipated for us. And we were not the fastest runners, either, especially Steven who generally avoided activities requiring any physical exertion or stamina. Even in his childhood he was on the heavy side.

The bull or cow or whatever it was never made a move for us during all of our adventures at Spy Rock, but this experience was often the high point of our day.

* * *

Paul and I kept in touch with Steven long after our daily adventures had ended. For us, Steven Moore was the only reason to venture back to Newboro. A life-long friend, he was always happy to see us and always willing to sit and chat, or perhaps even participate in another adventure. We would camp on one of the islands with Steven, drinking beer and rye this time, cooking food over an open fire while listening to music but still maintaining that same sense of mutual respect. Steven never left the Rideau Lakes area, working in restaurants in Westport or Newboro for much of his adult life.

Every time we returned to see Steven he would be heavier. He ate junk food most of the time, especially his beloved Pepsi and chips. I don't ever remember seeing Steven eat any fruit or vegetables.

At the age of 36 and weighing close to 300 lbs, Steven Moore died in his sleep. He nodded off in his chair while watching television in his apartment in Westport. A friend discovered his body the next day. The coroner concluded that Steven's death could be attributed to sleep apnea, an ailment he never knew he had.

* * *

One more incident, and this is typical of Steven and his influence on us, took place at Steven's funeral. Paul and I were upset when we found out about his early death. Like all early deaths it made no sense. The funeral was scheduled for a Tuesday in early October. I was to meet Paul and my mother for lunch at a restaurant in Westport and then we'd go on together to the funeral chapel.

At lunch we talked about Steven and shared stories. The waitress that day also knew Steven, as did everyone else in Westport, and she shared her stories. It was a fitting tribute to the man and the ideal setting for this as well. But we still had to go to the chapel for the official send off.

As we were leaving the restaurant, I mentioned to my mom that she should sit between Paul and me. Sometimes in moments of heightened emotion Paul and I lacked maturity. For example, we used to have this problem with "church burps". You know the kind: the deep-throated ones that escape during an extended yawn and usually at the quietest point of the service. Silence amplified the volume of this church burp, and then we would both break out in furtive fits of laughter, embarrassing our dad and God himself in the process. We were older now and the likelihood of one or both of us breaking out in uncontrollable fits of laughter was minimal. Still, it seemed wise to take precautions. My mother agreed to sit between us.

We arrived at the chapel just as the procession line was ending. We were the last people through to express our sympathies to Steven's family. They were all there and lined up in front of the casket, on top of which was a photo of a smiling Steven. It was very emotional. It hit me that my childhood friend who I had known for almost 30 years was gone.

I embraced his older sister Louise, and she whispered to me that she had a picture of Paul and Steven together and that she would like to give the photo to Paul at the gathering afterwards in Newboro. I smiled and nodded. Then it was time to find our seats.

Because we were the last ones in the chapel, we could not find three seats together anywhere. My mother found a seat off by herself. Paul and I headed to two open seats near the front of the chapel. I sat directly beside Paul. We were one row from the front of the chapel.

This was not good. I was not only upset about Steven; I was now anxious about sitting next to Paul. Then I made the fatal error.

I leaned over and whispered to Paul: "Louise said that she has a picture of you and Steven and that she would like to give it to you."
"What?" was his surprised response.
"A picture, of you and Steven . . . Louise has a picture of the two of you. She wants to give it to you."

He put his head down.
Oh no, I thought, *here we go.*
Paul started to crack a smile, as did I.
Okay it's just a smile, I reminded myself.

Paul began to breathe heavily through his nose; his amusement with the statement was not going to end at just a smile. His breathing intensified as he tried to contain his laughter and nerves.

What was it that is so funny anyway? I wondered, as I felt laughter coming on.

Paul's heavy breathing turned into a full body shake, watering eyes and a beet-red face. My symptoms weren't much different.

This isn't good at all, I thought.

Here we were at a funeral of a close friend, and we were both losing our composure in front of everyone. Paul's convulsions intensified as did my feeling of helplessness. The people in front of us glanced over their shoulders. The people on either side of us turned their heads. The urge to explode in laughter wasn't going away.

As the preacher was droning on about Steven and all the lives he had touched, Paul stood up, his face bright red and tears streaming down his face. He made his way to the center aisle. Covering his face he speed-walked to the back of the chapel through the gauntlet of 100 or so mourners and exited through the back door. Paul's symptoms were no different from someone overcome by grief and to many that day this is how it looked—one of Steven's closest friends so distraught that he had to leave the chapel in tears.

With Paul gone, I was able to regain my self-control and follow along with the rest of the congregation that day in an appropriate mournful manner.

Meanwhile, immature and disrespectful Paul was too mortified to re-enter the chapel, so he remained in the parking lot until the service was over. Because of his embarrassment we never did make it to the reception that followed, and we never did get to see that now infamous photo of Steven and Paul. The funeral unfolded just as Steven would have liked as he, Paul and I shared one last laugh.

Country Squire

My dad enjoyed masquerading as an undercover cop. A guest at the lodge, a retired county sheriff from Pennsylvania, once presented him with an honourary sheriff's badge. My father elected to ignore the word "honourary". He carried a red magnetic cop light in his car. He had a citizens' band (CB) radio in the family car and in The Poplars' pick-up truck. As well, his home base in his office contained a complicated short wave, intercom and CB system.

His CB handle was *Country Squire,* partly because that was the style of car he drove, the elongated station wagon with fake wood panels on the side, the kind that would float down the road without ever coming in contact with the pavement. And I think he chose this moniker because it had a noble quality to it.

* * *

Also known as R.P. (Robert Patrick) among his closest friends, my father had everything but actual credentials to be a police officer. There was nothing he enjoyed more (with the exception of golf) than riding around in OPP cruisers in the middle of the night looking for fraudulent guests who had defaulted on payments, stolen something or in rare cases failed to show up at the lodge for their designated reservation dates during peak season.

Throughout the 70s he had my brother and me convinced that he was the pilot who landed the vintage T-6 Harvard war plane in Centennial Park in Smith Falls. It could have been true I suppose, but he claimed he landed the aircraft directly on the cement support platform. I would prefer not to use the term stupid to describe Paul and me at that time; gullible is more accurate.

He was an imposing man, six feet and 200 lbs, handsome with a strong jaw, full head of hair and broad shoulders. He looked like a cop, acted like a cop, talked like a cop. When he was wearing his sun glasses he even had his family convinced that he was an undercover officer. He was a restless man, and living in this fantasy world of law enforcement must have been an exciting escape for him.

*   *   *

My dad was everything I wanted him to be. I remember once giving him grief for not playing road hockey with my brother and me. A friend was visiting at the time. My dad said he was busy with something else, and he couldn't play hockey with us. Then he went inside. And I started to pout. My friend piped up and said, "Hey, you are lucky. My dad never does stuff with me. Your dad is always playing games with you two." This stuck with me.

Early on at the lodge my father became notorious for his magical and well-timed disappearing acts. In moments of high emotion and crisis somehow my dad would vanish and let my mother deal with the fallout. In fairness to my father, it may have been an unusual number of coincidences that led to this reputation. This phantom act used to drive my mother crazy.

My dad liked people, but on his terms. In the tourism industry, tolerating paying customers is a prerequisite, and most of the time my dad practised this very basic tourism tenet. He was the public relations guy at the lodge. My mom would work behind the scenes; my dad would be the face of the lodge. He had a personality and a humour that drew people to him. Everyone liked my dad, and he had few enemies, except for those of the imaginary kind. Most secret agents live in fear of their true identity being uncovered. What if the guests discovered that occasionally my dad didn't want to be around them? He couldn't allow that to happen.

RUNNING THE SHEETS

At the front desk of the lodge my dad loomed large, holding court with three or four guests at a time, telling stories, tall tales mostly, about gigantic fish in the lake or his latest sub-70 round of golf.

He was a classic kidder and knew just what to say to loosen up even the most uptight guest. There were a number of guests who came to the lodge from Brooklyn, New York each year. While the husbands just wanted to get away and fish, their wives were into a more complete experience. Everything had to be just right for the princesses from Brooklyn. They would complain about the beds, the linens, the food, the weather, the beds again, the food again, but by the time they had finished venting my dad would have charmed them back to reality. They would walk away having forgotten what they were complaining about.

As much as he enjoyed the daily interaction with the guests, he could only take so much. There were times, more frequent as the summers wore on, that he just wanted to be left alone and be allowed to go off and to do his own thing. Wanting to do your own thing and being able to do your own thing are two separate realities, especially in the resort business.

For five months every year his time was not his own, unless he took drastic measures. For R.P. this meant an elaborate plan of escape and disappearance that he would employ almost daily when he had had enough of needy guests and uninspired staff.

His covert disappearing acts were Houdini-like. He would stroll into the kitchen at a busy time or between meals. He would chat up the kitchen staff, joking, keeping the mood light and trying not to bring attention to himself. The staff would be either busy or laughing or busy laughing depending upon my father's topic of the day. Before anyone noticed, he was gone. He would slip out the back door of the kitchen and begin his stealthy saunter up the side of the property. It was impossible for him to escape via the main sidewalk of the lodge, because the guests were everywhere—picture a George Romero zombie movie.

This back-door escape route became his salvation. Making sure to stay close to the tree line, he would crouch low and vigilantly work his way up past the garbage room and the wood pile to the laundry room. If he made it to the rear of the laundry room he was home free. He could dart across the parking lot to the safety of our house or, even safer, his

Chevy wagon—not as romantic as an Aston Martin two-seater, but he was a secret agent. A wood-paneled station wagon was an ingenious cover.

If this route was blocked, he would continue his trek along the white-picket fence past the old log cabin, also known as the honeymoon suite, and stay glued to the line of poplar trees that followed the narrow gravel road to the top of the hill and By Street. From there he would hurry along the sidewalk to the house or his car. He was gone for hours only to reappear in the darkness to make his final rounds of the property.

* * *

My bedtime when I was a kid at the lodge varied in the summer months, but during the school year even when the lodge was open for business I had to be in bed between 8 and 9 PM every night. There were rarely any exceptions to this school night rule, except when the Stanley Cup playoffs were on TV and the Montreal Canadiens were in the final.

The short tradition of late night hockey playoffs at the lodge started in the spring of 1976 and continued in 1977.

In early May each year, my parents moved the large RCA floor model coloured TV from our family room to the social area of the main lodge. We were left with a smaller black and white TV in its place, but as the weather improved TV watching became less appealing. In the main lodge, the coloured television was used infrequently. However, the guest rooms were without televisions, so my parents felt it necessary to have the TV available for guests, even though we only received two channels: CBS from Watertown and CBC from Kingston.

In the spring of 1976, the Canadiens and Flyers were set to play for the Stanley Cup. The Canadiens had been in a drought by their standards and had not won the Cup in two seasons, so this was a chance for them to dethrone the two-time Cup champions from Philadelphia.

My dad was a passionate Habs' fan. At our house we cheered for all teams from Montreal whether football, hockey or baseball. My dad was an avid fan of all three, especially hockey. While he never demanded we support his beloved Canadiens, it was all we ever heard or saw in the house on radio or TV.

I had no problem cheering for the Canadiens and was soon equal to my dad in my knowledge of the game and of the players. Many Saturday nights throughout the winter we would sit together in the family room and cheer on our team. The bond between my dad and me was always strong, mainly thanks to our shared interest in sports and our mutual passion for the Montreal Canadiens.

The series between the Flyers and Canadiens in the spring of 76 was going to be a special one for us, our first time to share the excitement of a Stanley Cup final on equal terms. The dilemma, of course, was that the colour TV had been moved to the main lodge. All we had at the house was the antiquated black and white model. This was a problem, so too was the bedtime issue. My mother decreed that my bedtime was 9 PM on school nights. What was I going to do? The thought of watching half a game did not appeal to me at all, especially half a game in black and white.

Thankfully, I didn't have to negotiate anything. My dad understood my uneasiness and negotiated a later bedtime for me. As he liked to remind us, perhaps he was really the boss after all. Paul was not interested in hockey, so he was not included in this decision. It was just my dad and me. Best of all, we would watch all the games of the final series in glorious colour, and we would have the TV and main lodge to ourselves.

For a few weeks in May, my dad and I sat in front of the console television every other night and watched the Montreal Canadiens' run for the Cup. No microwave popcorn. No pop or beer either. We celebrated every time our team scored and remained silent whenever the Flyers scored. We were riveted to the TV screen, with each pass, each shot, each save, each hit and each goal causing our heart rates to fluctuate wildly. We would hang on every word, every phrase uttered by play-by-play man extraordinaire Danny Gallivan and his sidekick Dick Irvin Jr.

Conversation between us was minimal as we knew talking would affect our concentration, which in turn could influence the outcome of the game. We were convinced that our being there, our watching the game, our commitment to our team played a role in the outcome of the game. If we didn't concentrate, if we weren't passionate, the team's play would suffer. The Habs needed both of us at our best. We accepted this responsibility with honour.

The Habs defeated the Flyers in four straight games. As the final seconds of that May 16th Cup-clinching game wound down at The Spectrum in Philadelphia, my dad and I started to breathe a lot easier. We had given so much to our team that we decided that it was safe to relax in the final moments when victory was certain. The horn blew. The Montreal Canadiens were Stanley Cup champions again.

We may have hugged, we may have cheered, we may have jumped up and down, we may have done all three; I don't remember. I know we did not high five each other as neither of us had ever heard of the silly gesture. I do recall how exhilarating it felt quietly celebrating in the lodge that May evening, just the two of us, as the Canadiens skated around Spectrum ice, Cup in hand, Queen's "We Are the Champions" blaring in the background. This is the fondest memory I have of my dad at the lodge.

Never Cry Wolf

Liberated from babysitters, my brother and I ventured beyond the boundaries of the resort property. This meant travelling by bicycle all over town. "All over'" is a bit misleading as we could bike the circumference of the town in ten minutes if we kept a consistent pace.

These destinations were many. The witches' house, the Snots' house, the graveyard road, Spy Rock, Vic's candy store/pool hall, the B&W railway bridge, the locks, the blockhouse, the abandoned dump and the list goes on.

Freedom meant responsibility too, and for me this was a summer paper route. I did not possess the fortitude to be a winter paperboy, but delivering newspapers around a metropolis of 310 people at the age of nine was an ideal summer job, offering money and, more important, status with the ladies.

My CCM bike was the Mustang style with the extended banana seat and the over-sized curved handle bars. I classified bike rides into two categories: business and pleasure, with the line between the two often blurred.

The summer of 1974 was unusually sunny from start to finish. Or at least I didn't notice the rainy days. My route, which consisted of 27 customers, was stretched all over town. One destination was a home on a hill next to a slimy, old boat launch, near where the road ended and Newboro Lake began, not far from the graveyard road Paul, Steven and I frequented.

This area was boggy and the water shallow, an ideal spot to launch a boat. I often biked by this place contemplating what would happen if I started at the top of the road and travelled down the hill pedaling as fast as I could before slicing into the water. I assumed that I would hydroplane for at least a couple feet before flying over the handle bars. I was a daredevil in mind only.

On this particular day, I was running late and preparing for some impatient customers. As I was cruising by the boat launch, I noticed two men sitting on the hood of a fancy car with a prominent front end and a white vinyl roof, a generic mode of transportation in the 70s. One of the men was short and stocky. He wore sunglasses, jeans, and cowboy boots. He surveyed the water furtively. He was wearing black leather gloves too.

Black leather gloves in the middle of summer.

From a distance his face seemed red. He appeared agitated. The other man was much taller, well over six feet, and wore denim jeans, a collared shirt, sunglasses, and a white cowboy hat. He wore black leather gloves too. His body language suggested he was more relaxed. His gaze was fixed on the lake and nothing else.

I was about to pedal up the hill away from the boat launch when the little guy turned quickly and shouted sharply in my direction.

"Eh, kid!" he yelled.

His accent was different, and he was not anyone I had seen in town before. He started to move toward me as I slowed my bike not knowing whether to run or hide. Before I could decide, he yelled again.

"Eh, kid, come over ere!"

I was afraid. Young kids, even in small towns, even in the 1970s, weren't supposed to talk to strangers, especially angry ones.

Instinct said run. Fear said freeze.

Naturally, I froze. The little man walked toward me. The bigger man turned and also began moving in my direction. He meandered. The little guy walked quickly, his boots clicking on the pavement as he moved.

The day was bright. They stood in front of me with the sun over their shoulders. I had to squint just to make out their silhouettes. The big one looked like a giant, while the short one looked like a Hungarian body builder. But even he was taller than I.

I am dead meat, I thought.

The little guy did all the talking. He asked me if I lived around here. He asked me what paper I delivered. He asked me how old I was. Then he demanded I give him one of my newspapers.

Being the idiot I am, I said, "I am sorry, Mister, but I do not have a newspaper to spare."

"Tabernac!" he declared, turning to his friend and shaking his head with a menacing smile. The big guy removed his eyes from me and stared out at the lake.

Tabernac? What the hell does that mean? I thought. And why does this guy talk so funny?

"Come on kid give us one paper, eh?"
"No, really, I can't."
"Yes you can and you will," he demanded. "You like money, don't you?
"Yes, Mister."
"Give us de paper. I pay you for it."

My mind cleared. All they wanted was a newspaper. They were even willing to pay for it. I reached into my bag, wishing I could pull out a gun. With gun in hand, I would transform instantly into confident Jimmy, paperboy/super hero, and send a message to all evil-doers who ever felt compelled to badger a kid with a pre-determined number of newspapers into selling them "just one". I would be the Rosa Parks of paperboys.

Instead, I pulled out a newspaper.

The little guy grabbed it from my hand and was about to turn and walk away when the big guy said, "Hey, pay de kid, will ya."

The little guy reached into his pocket, pulled out a five dollar bill and handed it to me.

"Ere, take dis and go buy anoter paper."

I pocketed the money. By the time I looked up they were walking back toward the lake, once again silhouetted by the sun. I waited and watched them move to the front of the car where the little guy proceeded to sit on the hood and open the paper while the big guy leaned against the car and resumed staring at the lake.

I jumped on my bike. I was shaken but content with the tip I received for one lousy paper. Besides I had three or four extra at home.

As I rode away, I looked back one last time. They were looking back at me. I started pedaling faster.

* * *

Early September. A Wednesday morning. My brother, sister and I were in school. My mom and dad were winding down at the lodge.

There were no instant tellers in 1974. The Royal Bank in Newboro was open every Monday and Wednesday back then. That Wednesday morning my dad had to visit the bank to make one of his bi-weekly deposits. The amount he had to deposit, $5000 cinched tight in a blue Crown Royal bag, was larger than usual because it contained the Labour Day receipts. He was always anxious when he had to make a deposit at the vintage red brick bank, which was constructed in 1903. Secret agents deposit money into impenetrable Swiss banks, not turn-of-the-century museums in rural Eastern Ontario.

On that sleepy September morning in 1974 as my dad was exiting the front door of the bank and walking down the steps, he observed two figures to his right walking in the direction of the bank. He began walking towards them.

RUNNING THE SHEETS

My dad didn't recognize the two men. In a town of 310 people, they stood out. One was short and stocky; the other was tall and lean. They wore cowboy hats, jeans, cowboy boots, and sunglasses.

As my dad came closer, he noticed they were wearing gloves, black leather. He passed them on the sidewalk. They nodded in his direction. My dad returned the nod and headed down the hill to Louie Moore's house. After they passed him, my dad didn't look back, but he heard the clicking sound of their boots on the concrete and the thud of the heavy bank door opening and shutting.

Finally, after all these years, his moment had come. Every secret agent gets one career defining moment. This was my dad's. He had no intention of letting it pass. Years of toiling away with Bell Canada and operating a fishing lodge, perfect covers for an international man of intrigue, were now about to pay huge dividends. It was payback time.

My dad picked up his pace. When he arrived at Louie Moore's house, he knocked on the front door. Ethel, Louie's wife and mother of eight kids, came to the door.

My dad: "Ethel, there's a bank job about to go down in broad daylight."
Ethel: "Pat, have you been drinking?"
My dad: "Ethel, I am serious. I need to use your phone. We don't have much time."
Ethel: "Pat, don't you have something better to do than play practical jokes all day? You are a respected businessman in this town."
My dad: "Please, Ethel, I need to use your phone."
Ethel: "Pat, I am watching my program . . . Go bother someone else."

Ethel Moore had been the victim of many of my dad's practical jokes. She refused to believe his wild story. She also refused to let him in her house. Not that it would have helped. The Moores didn't own a phone.

Discouraged, my dad crossed the street. He headed in the direction of Jack Williams' Superior Propane filling station, located across the street from the bank. His paced quickened. He noticed a propane truck parked in front of Jack's place. Off to the side of the building he saw two large propane storage tanks. His mind began to race. He had to get to Jack's, to a phone. He started to run, all the while keeping a close eye on the front door of the bank.

As my dad entered the front door of the propane station, he found Jack sitting at his desk by the large window on the right. Jack was smoking and pounding an adding machine. According to my father, here is how the conversation went:

My dad: "Jack, the bank's being robbed! Can I use your phone?"
Jack: "Are you serious, Pat?"
My dad: "Dead serious, Jack. I just saw two guys go into the bank wearing leather gloves."
Jack: "Here's the phone. I'll get my shotgun."
My dad: "What? Jack, do you really think that is a good idea?"
Jack: "Why not? It's just in the backroom. It's already loaded. It's double barrel, too."
My dad: "Jack, this is a propane station. Do you want to get into a shootout with these guys? They look like real pros . . ."
Jack: "I don't care. Those bastards are robbing the bank with my fuckin' money in it. They've got to be stopped."
My dad: "Not by us, Jack—by the cops."
Jack: "It will take forever for the cops to get here. We have to handle it ourselves."

My dad and Jack crouched down low by the window. They had a perfect view of the bank. Jack cocked his shotgun. He was ready to open fire. My dad pleaded with him not to pull the trigger. Drummond Street was eerily still. They waited.

Jack: "When they get to the sidewalk, I am going to start shooting . . . Shit! There they are!"

Jack sees the bank robbers peering out the front door of the bank. First the head of the little guy then the head of the big guy. The door opens slowly. They move swiftly down the steps, bags of money in hand. Their pace quickens. The street is deserted. They each glance back at the bank. There is no activity.

Across the street at the propane station everything is still. Jack holds his gun tightly, but he doesn't pull the trigger as the robbers disappear into their car and speed away.

My dad finally makes the phone call. Twenty minutes later, the police arrive.

Later that week, the Ontario Provincial Police find the getaway car in a quarry 30 miles away. Thanks in part to my dad's description, the police capture the two men a couple months later after they pull another bank job somewhere in Quebec. Their trial for the Newboro heist commences the following spring in Brockville. My dad is one of the lead witnesses for the prosecution. The judge sentences the two bank robbers to ten years for armed robbery.

It was years later after talking to my dad about his experience that I made the connection to the two men I encountered by the edge of the lake that August afternoon. The bandits did not touch my father's $5000 Crown Royal bag deposit. The police discovered the bag just inside the teller's wicket. One of the tellers pushed it aside just as the bank robbers announced their intentions. The investigators even hinted at my dad's possible involvement in the caper because of this fortunate turn of events. Of course, they had no idea my dad was a government operative. Nor was he about to reveal his true identity.

Das Boot

Many memorable events at the lodge occurred around the July 4th holiday. Next to June 25th, which was the official opening of bass fishing season (and my dad's birthday, which he reminded guests at any opportunity), July 4th was the most anticipated date of the year.

July 4th meant Americans, parades, fireworks, speed boat races, cookouts, mayhem, and . . . my brother Paul's birthday. My parents were busy on July 4th. Consequently, Paul's birthday was a hurried after-thought with cake, a few friends and some gifts. It was over in less than an hour.

Paul never complained, but his birthdays were uninspired. He had every right to lay charges of neglect against my parents, but the children's lobby was not as powerful as it is today. Consider the pressure to provide fancy loot bags at today's birthday parties. Do you think this just happened? The loot bag phenomenon required extensive lobbying on the part of children and their advocates back in the early 1980s. Today, the tragedy is in having inadequate loot bags, not in having a birthday party cut short because of time constraints or other commitments.

My brother's birthday parties were forgettable, but July 4th was not.

I recall one that fell on a Saturday, which translated into more chaos than usual because Saturdays were also a time for the weekly cookouts on the main lawn. Guests, staff and we kids all looked forward to these cookouts.

My parents dreaded these events because they were weather dependent. Once in a while, a sudden thunder storm destroyed the celebratory mood of the crowd gathered for the occasion. Guests ran for cover to the shelter of the main lodge with dinner and beverage in hand. Frenzied kitchen staff transported pots of food, bowls of salad, plates of cooked meats, layers of desserts, and piles of table cloths to the safety of the lodge dining room.

But most Saturdays in July were sunny, warm and pleasant. This is how it was on a particular Saturday in July when something went wrong at the waterfront.

Tables and chairs blanketed the main lawn. Ravenous guests sat and devoured the fine cuisine the lodge kitchen had to offer. Servers wormed their way through the tables offering refills and seconds of everything. Everyone seemed content. No complaints about the food. No complaints about the service. The weather was perfect, the bugs non-existent. It couldn't have been better.

At the main dock, Louie was busy filling the gas tanks of a larger pleasure craft. The vessel belonged to a family of six from Toronto. After Louie pumped the last drop of gas, he accepted payment. The family and their pleasure craft were ready to set out onto the lake to continue their journey. The four kids and the mother were stretching their legs on the dock waiting for Louie to return with their credit card and gas receipt. The father was in the driver's seat of the boat. At the turn of the ignition key, the serene atmosphere of a Saturday in July at The Poplars changed dramatically.

My brother and I sat on the edge of the sidewalk eating hamburgers and sipping lemonade when it happened. We were in our usual oblivious-to-everything state and were more concerned about the availability of condiments than anything else.

Then we heard it. Kaboom! The back end of the boat exploded. Flames shot high into the air. Immediately, dense black smoke billowed from the rear of the boat.

We had front row seats for our first ever exploding boat show. The multiple explosions created an impressive pyrotechnics display. We were mesmerized by the spectacle. We weren't sure what to do. The guests sitting at tables on the lawn eating their dinners let out a collective shriek. They sat motionless for a moment as the horrifying scene unfolded.

All around us staff and guests started to scramble, running in various directions. The screams intensified. Normally serene fishermen were transformed into drill sergeants, shouting out orders to anyone who would listen. It could have been a scene out of any 1970s disaster film, *Airport, Towering Inferno, The Poseidon Adventure*—pick one. It could be called *Pleasure Craft Calamity*.

For Paul and me, it was dinner theatre. We remained seated, out of fear or wonder, savouring our burgers and enjoying the show. We were too young to know what to do.

Another explosion and more flames and more smoke. More screams, more panic. The father jumped from the boat and pushed his distraught family toward the boathouse and the safety of the shoreline. More smoke billowed from the back of the boat. The flames shot higher.

Finishing my burger, I eyed my parents. They and the rest of the kitchen staff stood on the lawn, just in front of Paul and me, transfixed by the image of the burning boat. My parents' faces revealed the seriousness of the moment. My mother's face was frozen, eyes and mouth open wide. My dad stood motionless, mouth closed, eyes fixed on the burning boat.

The boat was not going to stop burning any time soon. The boathouse fire extinguisher was no match for the expanding inferno.

My father thought beyond the burning boat. The boat was aflame next to the dock, and it had not moved away from the dock. On the dock was the gas pump, and running along the bottom of the dock was the gas line. This gas line ran all the way up the side of the lodge property to the tank at the top of the hill. The potential for disaster was real, especially if the gas line was ignited. The entire place could go up in flames.

R.P. decided it was prudent to evacuate the area. I heard more emotion in his voice than I had ever heard before, even more than when he was reprimanding Paul for sniffing propane, drinking turpentine or consuming a large goblet of bourbon and mix when he was seven and no one was watching (his slurred speech after the fact gave it away).

"Everyone leave the front lawn immediately. Move quickly to the road at the top of the hill. . . and remain calm," my dad shouted.

With my dad in the role of Moses, a mass exodus from the front lawn of the lodge commenced.

Guests and staff, young and old, dashed up the hill toward the parking lot. I still recall their faces. I remember the man from the boat, his face blackened, running up the hill carrying his youngest child, a little boy. The rest of his family followed, the two young girls inconsolable in their mother's firm grip.

My mother panicked as the evacuees ran past her. She was looking around the main lawn. She was looking for someone. Her eyes narrowed as she squinted through the smoky haze. She was looking for Paul and me who she assumed would be right next to the burning boat or worse, floating in the lake.

She yelled our names. She screamed our names.

She did not realize we were standing behind her. Paul tugged on the back of her dress. She turned, grabbed us by the wrists and dragged us up the hill toward the parking lot.

I looked back once or twice and saw clouds of black smoke blanketing the waterfront. I heard more explosions, muffled this time. The sky was dark. Inside our house, we peered out the panoramic picture window. Thick black smoke blanketed the buildings below. No human forms were visible.

There wasn't a fire department or fire fighting system in Newboro when we owned The Poplars. Still isn't today. It was too expensive for each small community to have its own fire truck. There were plenty of volunteers, but without the truck they were useless. The closest fire truck was five miles away in Westport. By the time it arrived at the lodge, the place would be up in smoke. There were also no fire boats in the area, so a fire on a boat on the water would just have to burn out over time.

We didn't realize it until later, but a split second decision made by Louie Moore, the handyman extraordinaire and the hero of many stories, saved the lodge from destruction.

Louie stood calmly on the main dock, assessed the situation and acted. Fires represented nothing new for Louie. Once while driving from Brockville to Newboro, he noticed a house fire just outside the town of Delta. It was late at night. There were no lights on in the house. Smoke oozed out of one of the upper windows.

Louie pulled in the driveway, jumped out of his car, and ran into the house. Inside, the family of five was sound asleep. They were awakened by Louie's urgent shouts. Louie made sure all occupants of the house were safely outside and that someone had called the fire department. He refused to stick around for any acknowledgment from either the family or the fire department.

This quiet departure was part of Louie's character; fanfare was not important to him. It turned out that Louie was also driving without a driver's licence, so his hasty departure could have served another purpose as well.

On the dock, Louie realized that he had to get the boat away from the dock and the gas pump. Grabbing an oar from a nearby boat, Louie pushed the burning boat away from the dock. The entire area was enveloped in black acrid smoke, and it is hard to imagine how Louie could see clearly, let alone think clearly. But he did, and his actions saved the lodge from disaster.

Louie Moore at the waterfront

Once Louie pushed the boat away from the dock, the wind somehow—divine intervention is what my mom and dad later called it—shifted and the boat drifted out to the middle of the bay. There it continued to burn for another hour, eventually disappearing into the depths of the lake.

Louie refused to accept credit for saving the day, but his action was the primary reason the lodge was left standing after the explosion at the waterfront. Later, the fire marshal concluded that there was a leak in one of the gas tanks in the back end of the boat. Because it had an inboard motor this leak was undetectable. The flash from the spark plug ignited the gas fumes.

I now had something new to add to my ever-growing worry list: in-board motors. I paid attention to the main dock every time one of these boats came in for a fill-up.

Crazy Greg

Most of our childhood friends had two parents at home. The concepts of separation and divorce were foreign to us.

Greg Childs was the first kid we knew who didn't have both parents at home. His mom's name was Sylvia, and she could handle the jobs of mother and father. She was a strong, confident and assertive woman who always put the welfare of her son first. She held many different jobs and worked part time as a waitress at the lodge. It was rumoured that she once split a two-by-four over her knee. She never denied this.

When we first met Greg, he informed us that he had participated in a hot-air balloon race between Newboro and Portland, a neighbouring town ten miles away. He boasted that he competed solo in the under ten category, and he finished first. He didn't indicate how many other kids were in the under ten category.

We believed him at first because he told the story of the balloon race with conviction. However, the absurdity of an eight year old competing in and winning a hot air balloon race quickly became clear to us. Even more absurd was the idea of having a hot air balloon race between Portland and Newboro, which combined had a population of 600 people.

We called Greg on this blatant lie. He eventually admitted that it was untrue and that he just felt the need to impress us on our first meeting.

This was the beginning of our friendship with Greg Childs. We were always a little skeptical of anything Greg told us.

Greg, likely because he was an only child, had the most amazing kids' stuff. He had all varieties of models, toy soldiers, toy cars, toy trucks, Lego and board games. His bedroom was one of our favourite places to hang out because he regularly had new gadgets, and he was more than willing to share his stuff with Paul and me. His most prized possessions were his trading cards, mainly hockey and baseball. He also owned some black and white Beatles' trading cards, in mint condition.

It was 1974. Weekly, rumours circulated that the band was going to reunite. Even in the early 1970s the band's musical legacy was well established and their importance to the evolution of rock and roll well documented.

I suppose some kid in a small town in Ontario owning 20 Beatles' trading cards was no big deal, but my opportunistic younger sibling paid special attention to these cards every time we visited Greg. Paul frequently wanted to examine these cards, counting and recounting them at every opportunity.

Very early in life, Paul revealed a keen understanding of the value of things, especially items that no one else saw any value in. In the old dump on a hill in a wooded area near our house, Paul, Steven and I used to go hunting for bottles so we could smash them against the limestone ledges of the dump. Paul realized the stupidity of what we were doing and demanded we stop destroying the bottles. Intuitively, he understood the value of old medicine and pop bottles from the 20s, 30s, 40s, and 50s. Steven and I did not.

It was at this time that Paul began to collect antique bottles. Some bottles he discovered had significant value and were in collectors' books; one was worth close to $100—a Dr. Slocum's medicine bottle.

Paul had his sights set on Greg's Beatles' cards, but he didn't want to reveal their potential value to Greg.

One afternoon when we were at Greg's house and hanging out in his bedroom, Paul pulled out a Sweet Marie chocolate bar.

Greg: "Can I have a bite, Paul?"

Paul: "That depends."
Greg: "On what?"
Paul: "Are you willing to trade something for it?"
Greg: "For just one bite?"
Paul: "No, for the whole chocolate bar."
Greg: "What do you want for it?"

Paul surveyed the room, paced around a bit and came upon the cigar box where Greg kept his trading cards. He opened up the box and shuffled through the pile of hockey and baseball cards until he came upon The Beatles' cards secured tightly in a rubber band. He removed the cards from the box.

Paul: "How about these Beatle cards for the chocolate bar?"
Greg: "I don't know . . . my dad gave them to me."
Paul: "It's a good deal, Greg. Trust me. These cards are old. Plus, who cares about The Beatles anymore?"
Greg: "I don't even like The Beatles."
Paul: "Me neither."
Greg: "Deal."

It was over in less than 30 seconds. Paul had his cards. Greg devoured his chocolate bar.

I sat there and observed the swiftness of my brother's pounce. I had new respect for Paul, the master manipulator, and his astute eye for the value of things.

This ability would set him up nicely for a lifetime of treasure hunting in and around the Rideau Lakes area. Later, he would open up his own antique business in Brockville and sell numerous items he had discovered and paid a pittance for to treasure hunters all over the world on eBay. To this day he has The Beatles' cards stashed away somewhere, but he refuses to tell me where.

* * *

Greg Childs often felt the need to impress us. Whether it was his toy collection, his hot air balloon exploits, or his fearless feats on his bicycle, Greg was never content just being an ordinary kid doing ordinary things. He would try various stunts with his many bikes. It seemed that Greg would get a brand new bike every year, possibly a gift from his father who exited stage left when Greg was a baby.

He would ride his bike down stairs, he would pop wheelies, he would pedal as fast as he could and slam on the brakes in an attempt to leave the longest skid mark. At the end of every year his bike was beat up from all the stunts he had tried. He didn't care about the condition of his bike, however. He was more concerned about being accepted and included.

One day while riding down the steep hill close to our house, Greg noticed a rocky ledge and drop-off to the left, roughly half way down the hill. He stopped his bike and dismounted. He motioned for Paul and me to come over. The drop-off from the top of the ledge to the grassy ditch below was about ten feet. Right away, we knew what Greg had in mind.

He was determined to ride his bike off the edge and land fully intact in the high grass in the ditch below.

But it wasn't going to happen right away. Greg needed to survey the landing area first and make sure that it was suitable for a smooth landing. He told us that he wanted to do the jump before a live audience, which meant more than just Paul and me.

We spent the next half hour biking around Newboro announcing to anyone who would listen that Greg was going to ride his bike off a rock cliff and land it in the grass below. Most people ignored us, but we were able to convince Steven Moore and a couple other kids to attend the showcase of Greg's jumping talents.

The moment arrived for Greg Childs' jump. It wasn't daredevil Ken Carter attempting to jump the St. Lawrence River in a rocket car in 1981. It wasn't even close. But it was at least something to liven up a dull summer day in Newboro.

At the time, Greg owned a brand new three speed Supercycle bike, the kind that looked like a ten speed with the rounded handle bars and the skinny tires. It was mustard yellow and in pristine condition. He had had the bike for less than a week. It was not suited for any kind of stunt, especially a jump off a ten-foot cliff.

Greg didn't seem to care about his bike; he was more focussed on completing the stunt in front of his peers.

I suppose Paul or I should have said something like, "Greg, this is insane. You could wreck your bike or, more likely, you could really injure yourself. You don't have to do this to impress us or anyone, Greg. Don't do it, Greg!"

We didn't say anything to stop him. I don't think we thought of saying anything to him. This was his stunt. We were looking forward to witnessing history or tragedy in the making.

We picked a spot on the hill next to the jump site and sat down to wait for the show to start. There was a carnival atmosphere. We shared some what-if scenarios, our conversations sprinkled with nervous laughter. What if he crashes horribly and ends up a mangled mess? Who is going to tell his mother? Our mothers? Will we all be held accountable?

Or worse . . . what if Greg clears the jump and lands it perfectly? Will he be even more insufferable than usual? Will his success legitimize his many fictitious feats? There were many questions and no clear answers.

The anticipation was palpable; the atmosphere electric. Someone commented that we should have packed a picnic lunch. It was a beautiful sunny day in early July, so a picnic was a great idea. But it was too late for that. Greg had taken his spot at the designated starting point at the top of Moss Cliff.

A quick wave of the hand indicated he was ready. He began his approach. He started pedaling slowly at first; probably because he had his bike in third gear, and then he began to pick up speed. He was pedalling as fast as he could down the road, and it did occur to us at this point that either a) he would chicken out or b) he really might hurt himself. I think Paul may have expressed concern for Greg's well-being; I know I didn't.

Greg pedalled at top speed and started to veer left toward the jump site. It would only be a matter of seconds now before he was airborne. We crossed our fingers. No we didn't; that's a lie. We opened our eyes wide and waited for the inevitable. Before we knew it, Greg was soaring high above the grassy ditch below, his legs now flailing behind him parallel to his bike. His head was above and ahead of the handle bars. It was all he could do to just hang on. We gasped, winced and held our collective breaths. The landing was less than a second away. Perhaps the tall grass would cushion his fall.

Greg let go of the handle bars just before the front wheel of his bike collided with the ground. He flew over the handle bars and hit the ditch hard, really hard. He landed in such a way that his chest hit the ground first while he attempted to hold his head high to spare it from direct contact with the ground. His bike rolled a couple of times and came to rest on top of him. We sprang from our seats and scurried down the hill to the crash site.

We lifted Greg's mangled bike off him and found Greg face down in the dirt. He appeared to be injured. He wasn't moving, he wasn't talking, there was a cut above his eye, and his breathing seemed off. His chest heaved up and down as he struggled to find his breath. Any breath he did take was raspy and short.

As Greg Childs lay dying in the tall grass, I felt ashamed of my role in this fiasco. In the immortal words of postman Cliff Clavin from the television program *Cheers*, I was "ashamed God made me a man . . ." Carla's retort would have been appropriate too: "I don't think He's doing too much bragging about it either."

We assumed he was on his way to the great hereafter. We couldn't just sit there and watch him die, regardless of how cool that would have been. We sat him up, unaware of the possibility of spinal cord damage, and asked him if he was okay. He was not okay. His breathing was still laboured. He was in shock. We stood unmoving.

After another minute his breathing started to return to normal. He lay there with his head in his hands not saying anything as he focussed on his breathing. Finally, he looked up. We could see tears welling up in his eyes. He started to cry.

He was looking in the direction of his bike lying on the ground next to him. The front tire had taken the brunt of the impact and the front forks were bent at a 90 degree angle. The handle bars were twisted. His bike was not in rideable condition and would require significant repairs. Nothing we could say could stop the crying. We helped him up, picked up his bike and staggered out of the ditch together. At the top of the road, Greg, breathing normally now, asked for his bike and announced that he had to go home. He mumbled that his mother was going to kill him when she found out.

Greg Childs walked home alone that afternoon, dragging his wrecked three-speed beside him. Later that evening, Greg's irate mother phoned the parents of each kid who had witnessed the afternoon spectacle. She informed them of what happened and let everyone know that Greg was not to be performing dangerous stunts on his bike again. Through our parents, Sylvia scolded all of us and condemned our roles in the incident.

The legend of Crazy Greg was born.

The Witches' House

Not far from The Poplars, on a heavily treed lake-front lot, stood a beautiful two-story wood frame home. We often rode our bikes by this house and wondered who lived there or, by the looks of the place, who *used* to live there.

From the road it was a haunting image, barely visible and shrouded by over-hanging trees. The edges of the house were blurred, obscured by shadows and foliage. Whenever we garnered enough courage to trespass, the eerie silence of the place got to us before we could set foot on the property. It was more a part of nature than it was of civilization.

Built sometime in the 1920s, just like the main lodge at The Poplars, it had all the qualities of a stately summer home. The covered veranda that ran the length of the front and the side of the house was particularly appealing, as were the old Adirondack chairs that lined the porch. The white exterior and forest green trim and shutters enhanced the colonial appearance of the house. It had the potential to be one of the finest homes in Newboro.

However, time and neglect had diminished the house. It was in dire need of a paint job, and some of the trim and shutters required repair. The house was adjacent to the shoreline and positioned in such a way to provide an optimum view; however, the foliage of the overgrown trees and bushes negated any potential vistas of the lake. The lawn was uncut.

The remnants of a children's swing could be seen hanging precariously from an ancient oak in front of the house.

There was little evidence of life, other than the beat-up VW van hidden in the bushes. No laughter, no activity, no barbecues, no lawn darts . . . nothing. Daily we observed the same desolation. At night we could see the dark silhouette of the house enveloped by trees, but we never once saw a light in any of the windows. Later, we learned the house was without electricity.

This house became the mystery house on our regular tours of the town and the object of much fascination. To pass the time, we made up stories about this place. A nocturnal creature, half man, half fish lived there. The ghosts of the men who built the Rideau Canal took their breaks on the porch, leisurely reclining in the Adirondack chairs. They vanished whenever would-be intruders ventured up the lane. We never got close enough to verify any of our theories.

* * *

Early one summer two young girls, twins, with long dark curly hair, sleepy eyes and floral print dresses arrived in Newboro. We had never seen them before. They seemed withdrawn and timid whenever we saw them. Who would blame them? Newboro's kids weren't the most accepting even at the best of times.

These two girls were enigmas to us. Instead of making them feel welcome and including them in our games and adventures, we became suspicious of them. Perhaps because they were girls; but more likely because they were strangers to the town.

Emotional cruelty is a common currency of children. Growing up in a small town is no different. Either you fit in or you didn't. Small-town paranoia has a way of taking over an individual, even a kid. Residents of small towns fear change and often judge strangers quickly and harshly. While Paul and I were once strangers in this town, most of our peers accepted us. Familiarity was the key to this acceptance more than anything else. Curiosity soon replaced suspicion, which led to friendship. This process took time.

These phantom girls with the long dark hair were hampered by their newness. Nothing could be done to change this.

Soon after their arrival, they showed up on the bus to swimming lessons in Westport. They sat quietly while everyone around them—almost every kid between age 8 and 14 in Newboro—talked and laughed. The girls said nothing to anyone except the occasional whisper to each other. No one seemed to notice the girls directly, but everyone on the bus was aware of them. As a boy about the same age as these girls, I noticed them. There was nothing about them I found disagreeable. They possessed a natural beauty, in a youthful beatnik sort of way, a look which I have always found appealing. But this dreamy notion was soon replaced by a harsher image in my mind.

I am sure all eyes on the bus were on them at some point during the short journey, looking for anything, a weakness or a flaw that could be used as ammunition against the unsuspecting prey. Someone—it could have been anyone—sitting in the seat in front of these girls turned to look at them. It was a dead stare, penetrating and unnerving. Eventually this individual noticed something abnormal, something worth reporting to the others on the bus. It led to a finger point, a laugh, and a whisper. Within seconds, the news bulletin had spread through the entire bus.

Hanging from one of the girl's nostrils was a gooey yellow glob. Once exposed, this glob became her most prominent feature. Everything else faded . . . her beautiful hair, her seductive dark eyes, her porcelain skin . . . all were gone. In their place was the ever-expanding booger.

Any chance of a normal progression from suspicion, to curiosity and then to friendship had ended for these two girls. Allergies, a cold, a deviated septum . . . it didn't matter. She had snot hanging from her nose. The ridicule began immediately.

As always, Paul and I were certainly not the ringleaders of the cruelty; we also did not condemn anyone for it either. From that point on, the two girls on the bus and their entire family became known as "the Snots". The christening on the bus was permanent. To fit in, I joined the vocal chorus. *Better them than Paul or me*, I thought.

Snots! Snots! Snots!

The girls didn't say anything after they were humiliated on the bus. Every day for two weeks that summer they boarded the bus, took their seats, and stared out the window. After the swimming lessons ended each day, they faced the same ridicule and scrutiny on the return bus ride. The bus would drop everyone off on Drummond Street and the two of them, still nameless other than Snots, would hurry in the opposite direction of everyone else. Not once did they try to engage anyone in conversation and not once did anyone try to engage them.

As we discovered later, the twins were from New Jersey and their parents were hippies. At least they looked like how we thought hippies should look: long hair, pony tails, sandals. They had purchased the ghost house around the corner from our house to get away from the urban chaos of their winter home or, as some astute Newboro residents suggested, for the father to avoid the draft. They didn't need electricity; they didn't need a perfectly manicured lawn. As it turned out, they didn't need to be accepted by the community. They kept to themselves and probably would have even without the incident on the bus. All they wanted was peace. Perhaps the parents found this. I am not sure their daughters did.

* * *

Across the road from the twins' summer home was a much smaller one-story wood frame house. It was nestled in a stand of poplar and maple trees, but the house itself was visible from road. Secrecy surrounded this house as well; not so much because of its appearance but because of its inhabitants.

Three elderly sisters lived together in this tiny one-story house. We never saw them outside and were only aware that someone lived there because of the time we stopped there to collect money for *The Jerry Lewis Telethon* one Labour Day. They gave us a quarter for our cause but seemed put-out by the intrusion. From this brief encounter we learned that there were three of them. They looked alike, sisters we assumed, with white hair, old-fashioned dresses with high necks, and knitted shawls. One was stout, one was thin, and one was medium sized.

That was all we needed to know because our imaginations did the rest.

Because they were sisters, because they were really old, because we never saw them outside, because they lived in a tiny house in a wooded area, we, of course, concluded they were witches. Once we came to this conclusion, our daily bike rides down the hill and around the corner took on a more suspenseful quality.

At first it was our fascination with the Snots' house that drew us to this area; now it was a two-for-one special comprised of equal elements of fear, suspicion and curiosity.

We would stop our bikes on the narrow road between the two houses, first peering into the trees to search for any activity at the Snot household; then we would turn our attention to the witches' house, again looking for any evidence of life. The curtains were drawn so we could not see into the house; and it was not clear if there was any electrical power in the house either. There was no sign of life other than the odd piece of clothing, usually tattered old lady undergarments, hanging on the clothesline or the occasional wisp of smoke emanating from the chimney.

Smoke from the chimney.
Gotta be witches in there! we concluded.

Curiosity gave way to mischief as our passive voyeurism became tedious.

We, Steven, Paul, Barry Seed (another boy our age who we played with occasionally) and I decided to tempt fate to see what more we could find out about these reclusive witches. At the very least we needed to determine whether they were good witches or bad witches.

Barry Seed initiated the first attempt to discover more about the old women. He decided that he would simply go up to the house, knock on the door and ask for a quarter. At the time this seemed like a harmless thing to do, although 25 cents was a small fortune in 1975 – equivalent to $2 today.

Barry proceeded up the path to the wooden side door, actually the only door to the house, and knocked loudly. Seconds passed. No one answered. Barry knocked again, this time forcefully. After a couple seconds the door inched open. The stout one poked her head out.

"What do you want, my child?" she asked.
"May I have a quarter to buy some candy please, Ma'am?" Barry inquired.

The door closed in Barry's face only to be opened seconds later. This time with just the old lady's arm extended. She was pinching something between her boney fingers.

"Here," she said in a gruff voice. "Take this and don't come back again."

Barry grabbed the coin from the old woman's hand and ran back down the path to the road where we waited for him, bikes in hand and ready for a prompt escape if necessary. Barry wasn't smiling, but he wasn't frowning either. He had just made 25 cents, and all he'd had to do was to knock on somebody's door.

The rest of us resented this because most days Barry was not part of our adventures. He was not as obsessed with the witches' house as Steven, Paul and I were. He was not part of our railway bridge or Spy Rock exploits either. But he was not shy. Barry did what he had to do to get his candy fix, but it just didn't sit right with the rest of us, especially knowing that there was no way that he was going to share that quarter with us.

Many days passed before we decided to visit the witches again.

This time Steven, Paul and I—still feeling betrayed by Barry—were determined to get our fair share. The witches' house was part of our territory; and its inhabitants were our obsession not Barry's.

The three of us headed down Moss Cliff hill and around the corner in the direction of the witches' house. We stopped our bikes just past the house in front of the Snots and started to work on our plan. The best we could do was to duplicate Barry's plan from the previous week. We elected Paul to be the messenger this time because he was the youngest and easiest to persuade. He was also bravest.

At a distance, Steven and I remained mounted on our bikes as Paul dismounted his bike and lay it down near the ditch. We watched as Paul walked toward the path that led to the witches' house. He inched toward the door, his hands deep in his pockets and his eyes wide. He placed one foot on the step and then the other. He stared at the front door. He peered back at us. He stared at the front door.

But he didn't do anything.
"Come on, Paul, hurry up!" we pleaded, as quietly as we could.
Paul stood still. We whispered again. He stood motionless.

Finally, he moved toward the door and knocked three times. Then he turned and ran toward Steven and me.

"What is he doing?" I asked Steven, as Paul flew past us.

We watched as he mounted his bike. He pedalled by us without saying a word. Now we were frightened. We turned our bikes around and followed him.

Paul was directly in front of the Snots' house. He was pedalling as fast as he could. He didn't look back. Without warning, he and his bike came to an abrupt stop. Both flew up into the air and landed with a thud on the unforgiving asphalt. We raced to Paul and found him lying on the pavement, his bike resting on top of him. He wasn't crying; he wasn't saying anything. His was just lying there, his eyes open wide.

"Paul!" we shouted. "Are you okay?"

He didn't respond.

We climbed off our bikes and moved closer. Steven bent down and picked up Paul's bike. I kneeled at Paul's side.

"Paul," I said. "Are you okay?"
His head turned in my direction and in a quiet voice he asked, "What happened?"

I informed him that his bike had flipped and that he had hit the pavement hard. Steven and I helped him to his feet and righted his bike. There were no obvious signs of injury to Paul or of damage to his bike. The three of us got back on our bikes and decided to escape from the area as fast as we could. Our days of tormenting the witches and the Snots had ended.

Harry and the Go-Cart

My brother Paul used to be a terrible sleeper. When we were kids he would wake up in the middle of the night, sit up in his bed, point at the open closet door and let out a high-pitched scream, waking everyone in the house. I would hear Paul screaming, see him pointing at the dark opening of the closet and start shrieking as well. My mother would run in to console both of us, but mainly Paul because I usually was more embarrassed when she arrived than I was afraid. It would come out later that Paul had detected—once again—skeletons in the closet, their boney hands sliding along the edge of the open closet door.

I struggled with the fear level of skeletons. I didn't find them frightening at all. Plus the chances of having a skeleton in the closet are remote; goblins, bats, witches and, of course, monsters are more likely closet inhabitants. Sharing a room with my brother Paul for the first thirteen years of my life meant many abbreviated sleeps, and over time I became a very light sleeper because of this nightly ritual. Today, I wake up to even the slightest sound, thanks to my brother.

Paul's favourite colour when he was a kid was black. We didn't know this until one day his grade one teacher informed my parents of his choice. The class was engaged in the circle sharing activity and talking about favourites. Paul was the only kid who didn't choose a socially acceptable colour. Naturally, Paul's teacher informed my parents.

"So? There's nothing wrong with a few personality quirks," my mother responded.

However, with this innocent revelation the education system had something on Paul, and early on this combined with other peculiar personality traits and a penchant for drawing dark, disturbed pictures led to all sorts of trouble for Paul at school.

In grade one Paul was labelled as different because either consciously or subconsciously he chose not to conform. His learning style was more tactile than visual or auditory, and his teachers didn't recognize this. Paul was a more accomplished artist at age six than many kids twice his age.

Rather than adjust their methods, his teachers decreed that he required remediation to keep up with the rest of the class. When this didn't work they tried more drastic measures, first recommending professional help for Paul and then informing my parents in June of 1972 that Paul had failed grade one.

Failed grade one! How is that possible? How much does a kid have to piss off a teacher for this to happen? How could a teacher even consider doing this to a child at such a young age? The impact on Paul was devastating. The rationale? Paul was socially immature. Not academically, just socially. He liked black, and he was withdrawn and drew really scary pictures in class.

The following year, he had to repeat grade one with a group of strangers. His fragile self-esteem was completely shattered. Worst of all, his friends were moving on, and they soon found out that Paul wasn't. Paul was the kid who failed grade one; even some of his closest friends couldn't get past this unfortunate stigma.

As Paul's older brother, sometime best friend, sometime arch enemy, I had a choice to make. Either I would take the high road or I would use his failure as ammunition whenever the need arose. True to my nature, I chose to use it whenever things got at all heated between Paul and me. For me, his failure was a gift from God. And I used this gift often.

After my parents' initial warning to not to say anything, I began to use precisely timed strikes at moments when they were not around and Paul and I had had a dispute. Paul knew I possessed this winning card. No matter how well he fought physically or verbally in the end the "you failed grade one" line always won.

You'd think that after a while the reference would have lost meaning, but even into our early teenage years it was still as raw and cutting as it had ever been. Mercifully, he did not hold a grudge.

Of course, resilient Paul proved all the experts wrong. Not only did he complete the rest of his schooling on schedule he also went on to obtain two post-secondary degrees. He became an accomplished artist, an adept antique dealer and a social worker among other things. Very impressive stuff from a kid who was labelled early in his life as socially immature.

* * *

Paul was the original and spontaneous person I wished I was. From the beginning he seemed to know just what he wanted out of life. He loved the lodge environment more than any of us. He had more non-traditional hobbies and interests by the time he was ten than most adults. From an early age he was interested in collecting things, usually objects that to the uninformed eye seemed worthless. From old bottles to tin toys to the old glass insulators he discovered near the foot of derelict telephone poles, Paul uncovered many interesting treasures on his daily scavenger hunts around Newboro.

On mornings when we weren't awakened by Steven at our bedroom window, Paul and I would wake up early in the summer, sometimes to the sound of a low-flying loon, sometimes to the hum of an outboard motor and often to the aroma of breakfast bacon wafting up from the lodge kitchen.

We'd dress quickly. Paul would wear the same thing every day: a fisherman's cap with the extended beak, a flannel shirt and jeans. We would head our separate ways for a good part of the morning. Paul wore the fisherman's cap from sunup till sundown, but this came to an end one day when one of the guests informed him that if he continued to wear a hat all the time he would go bald. Paul discarded his worn-out fisherman's cap the very next day.

Paul set out seeking valuable collectibles and various creatures around The Poplars and the town. I ended up on the lawn in front of the main lodge sitting on the swing and gazing out at the lake. This was an important part of my morning ritual before the adventures of the day commenced. I would sit there by myself, hearing the occasional loon on the water, watching the departing fisherman in their boats, noticing the boats gassing up, and surveying the property and the pockets of activity around the lodge.

It was a tranquil time and my favourite time of the day; the lake in the morning was always at its most beautiful. The water was often motionless and glistened from the rising sun. The slightest movement, such as a jumping fish, set off a ripple that would last for some time. Then the stillness returned. I would await a new interruption, counting the minutes until the next splash or disruptive motor boat.

Paul and I would meet up later in the morning to see what he had collected and to plot our day's activities. Usually Paul had something interesting to show me.

One time he appeared with a small milk snake. I thought he, like I, was petrified of snakes, but he wasn't. I feigned interest but said that I didn't want to touch it. I was praying that Paul would not detect this weakness as it would give him some ammunition to use against me in times of civil strife. But he didn't think that way. I had nothing to fear. He kept the snake in a large glass relish jar with holes poked in the top. He put some grass and some dirt in the bottom, but other than that he didn't know what else a milk snake required in captivity.

Louie Moore informed Paul that insects were an important part of a snake's diet, so he started to feed the snake mosquitoes, flies and grasshoppers. He decided to name the snake Harry. Thus began Paul's unusual tradition of naming every pet he ever had Harry, whether it was a snake, a hamster, a goldfish or a bullfrog. There would even be some overlap in Harrys with Harry the snake living at the same time as Harry the hamster, so discussions with Paul about his pet Harry were always confusing. For example, how could a snake spend 20 minutes running on a wheel and then drink a whole cup of water? It was puzzling at the best of times when there was more than one living Harry.

There were epic funerals too. The Harrys died often, sometimes from neglect, sometimes by accident, rarely from old age. By the way, hamsters don't do well outside in the middle of winter. The funeral ceremonies were sombre affairs usually attended by most of our immediate family and even some guests and staff at the lodge. My mom or dad, again trying to compensate for Paul's inadequate 4th of July birthday parties, would say a word or two about Harry and then we'd bow our heads for a moment of silence before Harry was lowered into the ground in a shoebox and covered with dirt by Paul. But it wasn't that sad for anyone especially Paul who once the funeral service was over would be off to find a replacement Harry.

Many events stand out when I think of my brother Paul and our time together at the lodge. One of the more harrowing took place when Paul, Steven and I were having one of our daily planning sessions by an old poplar stump on the lawn in front of Broderick House, which was one of the larger guest houses and was named after my grandmother Kathleen Broderick.

We chose this spot for strategic reasons as it gave us a 360 degree view of our surroundings. We could never be too careful should a surprise attack be in the works. I was leaning on the old cement retaining wall next to the tree stump and Hazel, oops, I mean Steven, was beside me. Paul was sitting on the stump clad in his usual flannel shirt, fishing hat and jeans.

The meeting was going well, and we seemed to be in agreement on every issue when suddenly Paul stood up, a look of terror on his face. He pointed at his pants. Then he pulled up his pant leg. There must have been a least 20 yellow jackets, those fierce and aggressive little bees that attack in swarms, all over his leg. They had started to sting him.

Paul screamed. We screamed. Some of the bees raced toward Steven and me, but most stayed glued to Paul's legs hidden under the safety of his bell-bottom jeans.

Paul started to run. He made a beeline to the main lodge screaming like I had never heard him scream before. The intensity of his scream was ten times that of the middle of the night skeleton screams I had grown accustomed to. With Steven and me following closely behind, Paul crashed through the front door of the main lodge, raced through the front porch and living room areas, and ended up in the middle of the dining room where Poplars' patrons were enjoying lunch. The guests turned toward the noise, but they couldn't tell what was wrong because Paul's pant legs hid the evidence. Unable to talk, Paul stopped in the middle of the dining room. Still screaming, he proceeded to dance an Irish jig on the hardwood floor. The guests were transfixed.

My mother came out of the kitchen, expecting the worst.

Steven: "He sat on an old stump full of yellow jackets!"
Me: "There must be over 100 of them up his pants!"
Steven: "The bees are everywhere out there . . ."
Me: "We were swarmed."
Steven: "We got away, but it was too late for Paul."

One of the waitresses at the lodge, Viola Weir, pulled up one of Paul's pant legs to reveal the horrible sight. She picked him up and ran him into the kitchen, with my mother, Steven and me following closely behind. My parents considered Viola Weir to be the best waitress they ever had at the lodge. She always remained calm under pressure. This quality was evident on this day.

In the kitchen, Viola placed Paul on the bench beside the staff lunch table, pulled up both pant legs, and as quickly as they could, she and my mother began the painstaking task of yanking the bees off one at a time. Paul's chest heaved and tears ran down his face as they picked and squeezed. I thought he was a goner. He thought he was a goner.

With the bees removed, Paul's tears turned to sporadic sobs. His breathing returned to normal. He must have had over 25 bee stings. No one knew if he was allergic to bees.

My mother covered Paul's legs with a baking soda compound and spent the next 20 minutes observing him. Finally, she announced that he would survive. She was a nurse, and Viola had five kids of her own, so Paul was in expert hands. My mom took Paul to the house where he received some one-on-one attention.

Meanwhile, Steven and I discovered that we had been stung a couple of times too.

When we told Viola this, she handed us the bowl of baking soda compound. She informed us that she had guests waiting in the dining room and that we should take care of ourselves.

* * *

Another incident involving Paul took place on Labour Day of 1975 and involved an old wooden go-cart. We spent a good part of most of our summers riding our bikes everywhere: to the store, to the graveyard, to the old bridge. This was all we wanted—to have the freedom to bike wherever and whenever. We put hundreds of miles on our bikes every summer.

Near the middle of August we would tire of the monotony of the bike riding routine. So we began to consider other transportation possibilities.

We knew of one kid who lived on a farm outside of Newboro. He had taken an old, gas-powered lawnmower engine and hooked it up to his bicycle. This kid created the first motorized bicycle that we had heard of, somehow getting the rear tire to run off the lawnmower engine. But the engine was too powerful for his bike, and when he started it the bike did a wheelie and took off down the soft gravel road. Holding on with all his strength, the front wheel high in the air, this kid crashed into the ditch near his house. He was uninjured, but his bike was wrecked.

Inspired by this experiment, Paul, Steven and I explored other possibilities of powered transportation. We wanted something that didn't require any pedalling and also something that could hold more than one person. Naturally, we came up with the idea of using a large and flat square piece of heavy wood and attaching some boat trailer tires to it.

We concluded that this vehicle could carry up to six people. We considered designating it a tour train and charging tourists a fee for an historical tour of the town. One problem was the power source. We could use a lawnmower engine, but where would we obtain one? And we did have that kid's lawnmower fiasco in the back of our minds, plus our failed lawn-cutting business. Another problem was our lack of local historical knowledge. We could regale customers with stories of present-day Newboro; however, we would have to get creative when talking about Newboro's past.

Perhaps because we held most of our important meetings in the solitude of the laundry room, we decided that the most efficient means of propulsion for our yet to be designed vehicle would be to use an old wringer washing machine sitting unused in the laundry storage area. Why hadn't this gem of an idea occurred to us before?

We had our plan; we just needed to start construction on our vehicle and to get permission to use the old washing machine. There were some flaws in design and development. How did we expect to power this ELECTRIC washing machine, and how did we plan to convert it to something that could propel a tour train for six? Would we need a licence? Insurance? Seatbelts? Mercifully, the project never moved beyond the planning stages.

Our pursuit for other means of transportation did not end, however. We wanted something with four wheels. Something sexy, of course. On my paper route, I noticed a home-made wooden go-cart sitting in the bushes behind a shed at one of my customer's houses. It looked as if no one had driven it in years. I mentioned the go-cart to Paul when I returned home that day. He was eager to find out more. The next day he came with me on my route, and we stopped at the house with the go-cart.

Sid Galino, the woman who owned the house, also worked in the kitchen at the lodge. She, her husband and their four kids and one grandchild had lived in Newboro most of their lives. Sid was one of my parents' favourite employees. She was jovial and always a good sport about being the primary target of my dad's many practical jokes. Paul and I had a good relationship with her as well, which couldn't be said of all the kitchen staff some of whom found our presence in the kitchen annoying. Maybe they thought we were spying for our parents. Paul and I were confident we had an in with Sid.

The go-cart, despite years of disuse, was in pristine condition, made of sturdy plywood and painted dark yellow with black trim. It had good rubber tires, taken from an old Radio Flyer wagon, and even had a working steering wheel. It didn't, however, have any brakes . . . but who needs brakes in a small town like Newboro where there was only one significant hill?

The seed of desire was planted in Paul. He had a way of working on my parents. Usually my mother, who had a soft spot for Paul, gave in to his many requests. Because Paul was passionate and selective about the things he wanted and because he was well aware of my mother's weakness for him, he often received what he wanted. The dark yellow go-cart was no exception. Although it took a little longer than usual, he ended up the proud new owner of this vintage go-cart in August of 1975.

I do not know how I was left out of this deal. Was I not the one who located the vehicle? Was it not a joint desire to have a four wheel means of transportation? Was I not entitled to a finder's fee? Perhaps I said something at the time, perhaps not, but Paul made getting that go-cart his obsession that summer, and there was no way we would share its ownership.

Parental instructions to Paul and me were simple: Don't take the go-cart down Moss Cliff or the sidewalk that ran from the top of the hill at the lodge down to the lake.

Paul and I, well past the point when we should have been doing this, used to sit on our red Tonka toy dump trucks at the top of the main sidewalk, place our feet on the hood of the dump truck, and trundle down the hill toward the lake. We were able to control these dump trucks by just shifting our weight from one side to the other. The sound of the trucks' hard rubber tires tearing down the sidewalk would always get guests' attention, as would the sight of an over-grown child squeezed into the payload of a toy dump truck. We rarely crashed and were always able to veer off the sidewalk to safety before the cement bench and drop off to the lake at the end of the sidewalk.

The go-cart was a much larger vehicle, and for most of August we adhered to the rules our parents established. Either Paul would push me around in the go-cart; or I would push him. With minimum friction, the two of us made this agreement work. That is until the fateful night of Labour Day 1975.

The next day was the first day of school. After a summer of fantastic adventures and pseudo freedom, the thought of returning to the restrictive environment of school was not appealing for either of us. This was especially true for Paul. He hated school.

In the early evening on any Labour Day the sun seems to set earlier than usual, as if synchronized with the school year calendar. As the sun set on this day and darkness and shadows began to predominate, Paul and I sat at the crest of the hill where the main sidewalk began. Beside us was the go-cart, fading in the twilight.

With little discussion and even less thought, we decided that this was our time. This was the moment we would do what we had dreamt of doing for a good part of August. We would do what we had done many times with our asses jammed into the back of a Tonka dump truck. We would ride down the sidewalk from top to bottom in our four-wheel vehicle, and we would do this together. We had nothing to lose as school started the next morning. What were they going to do, ground us? Our lives were over as of tomorrow anyway.

Hastily, we developed a plan: Paul would drive and sit in the cockpit. I would sit on the back end of the go-cart feet tucked in behind him. I would hold on to his shoulders and navigate if necessary as I was higher up than he and would be able to see farther.

The sun had disappeared completely. Bats fluttered overhead. Fireflies glowed in the trees. There was some light coming from the front porch of the main lodge. If we squinted we could make out the outline of the sidewalk's edges. All we had to do once we passed the main lodge was to turn left or right off into the grass to avoid hitting the cement bench at the end of the sidewalk. We had done this hundreds of times in our Tonka trucks.

We started down the sidewalk hill, slowly at first and then began to pick up speed as we approached the steeper part of the hill in front of the main lodge. We were moving well. It was darker than we realized near the main lodge, but we remained on the sidewalk and were travelling at a good speed. Then, out of the corner of my myopic squinting eyes I saw something to the left of the sidewalk and on the lawn near the main lodge. I wasn't sure what it was at first. It was a silhouette of something familiar, something large and solid enough to do considerable damage to the go-cart and our heads.

It was the old, wooden wheelbarrow the busboys used to cart guests' luggage up and down the steep hill to the parking lot. It was usually parked just outside the entrance to the main lodge.

Why hadn't we remembered this? All we needed to do was to move it out of the way. But we didn't. Now we were in trouble. The two heavy wooden handles of the wheelbarrow were pointing in the direction of the lodge. They were at the exact height of my head as I crouched down behind Paul in the back of the go-cart. There would be no escape I thought. The go-cart was moving too fast. If Paul didn't see the wheelbarrow handles and turned to the left, I would be decapitated. I panicked and removed my hands from Paul's shoulders.

I grabbed for the steering wheel to prevent Paul from taking the left-hand bail out turn into the wheelbarrow. We fought for control of the steering wheel, pulling the go-cart from left to right and back again. We were doomed. I was doomed.

As Paul and I were struggling for control of the go-cart, I put my other hand around his head covering his face and obscuring his vision. We were approaching the main lodge and were now careening down the sidewalk fighting for control of the vehicle. Just as we came to the point on the sidewalk where the lodge was directly to our right, the go-cart took a sudden turn to the right. We were heading for the side of the screened in porch area of the main lodge. The outside of the main lodge was lined with overgrown hostas. At the entrance on either side of the screen door were two large cement planters full of impatiens and petunias in full bloom.

Paul managed to pull back enough on the steering wheel to avoid the side of the building, but the hostas were not as fortunate. We ploughed through these plants one by one, rising ever so higher as we scraped along the side of the wooden porch. We were now on two wheels with the right side of the go-cart elevated thanks to the accumulation of hostas underneath.

The go-cart was high enough for its underside to scrape violently over the top of one of the cement planters. The grating sound of the heavy wood of the go-cart hitting the first planter was deafening as we came to a dead stop between the two planters directly in front of the doorway. The go-cart leaned precariously on its left side while I clung to Paul's head. We remained frozen there for about five seconds. Perhaps it wasn't as loud as we had thought. Perhaps everyone was sleeping. Perhaps we could climb out of the go-cart, push it back up the hill and pretend the accident never happened. Or perhaps we could just face the music.

Sleepy guests came running out of their rooms. Other guests scurried out into the porch area of the main lodge, peering out into the night. Then my parents arrived on the scene, seeking in the darkness an explanation for the commotion. My dad moved to the porch door and squinted through the dark screen. There was just enough light at just the right angle coming from the porch lights that he could see our faces peering up at him from the toppled go-cart.

"Jesus Christ!" I remember him saying in a simmering voice. "What the hell have you two done now?"

We were blocking the entrance to the lodge. My dad, followed by my concerned mother, nudged open the screen door just enough so they could squeeze out. Once outside, they helped us from the overturned go-cart and asked us if we were hurt. My mother asked. My father said nothing. He didn't have to.

We were shaken up, we were embarrassed but we were not hurt. We stood up, our parents glaring at us, and surveyed the scene. The bank of hostas had been shredded. A large chunk of cement had broken off the top of the planter. There was a nasty gash on the underbody of the go-cart; otherwise, it was fully intact. Someone, somewhere sure knew how to make go-carts.

My father pushed the go-cart aside, and he ordered the two of us up the hill to the house. We walked slowly at first and then were joined by our mother who advised us to quicken our pace. Our father did not follow. After a hasty bath we were sent to bed. The summer of 1975 was over.

The Parade

The summer of 1976 produced more memorable events, many of which occurred around the July 4th celebrations that year when we were commemorating both the American bicentennial and the 100th anniversary of Newboro's official incorporation in 1876. With The Poplars populated primarily by Americans, there was little doubt which celebration would take priority.

The sincere love of country that many Americans possess is impressive. At a young age, I was aware that Americans were different from Canadians, even though they looked the same, albeit with greater access to all-you-can-eat buffets than we Canadians. Sure they had some strange accents whether they were from Brooklyn, New Jersey or Virginia, but they were similar to Canadians in many ways with one marked exception: They were openly proud of their country, their history, their soldiers, their war efforts, their God, their leaders, and, generally, of each other. The Vietnam War was into its second decade when we owned the lodge, and some guests had sons who had been or were still in Southeast Asia. Although the war was ever-present on the evening news, no one talked about it much, at least not when kids were within earshot.

To keep us out of trouble, our father who art on the golf course gave Paul and me the responsibility of lowering the Canadian and American flags at the end of the day and bringing these flags into the main lodge where we stored them behind the front desk. Sliding the flags down the flag poles proved to be a complicated endeavour for us as there were a number of ropes and hooks involved. Sometimes the flags would get caught half way down the pole, and we would have to get help from Louie. Other times, the flags wouldn't move at all and would stay on the flag pole overnight.

No one ever informed us of the tradition and importance of our task. We would lower the Canadian flag from one pole and the American from the other, drape the flags over our shoulders and run around the lawn disguised as undersized patriotic superheroes. We didn't treat the flags with respect; we just rolled them up in a ball, carried them to the lodge and threw them under the front desk.

An older guest, Ed Dean, a World War II veteran, took us aside one evening and gave us a crash course on flag traditions, respect and flag folding. He explained to Paul and me why it was important to respect a country's flag, and why it was wrong to run around with the flag or to do anything silly with it.

He proceeded to lay both flags out on the outdoor Ping-Pong table and show us how to fold a flag using small diagonal folds corner to corner instead of long straight folds. The flag was folded into a perfectly shaped triangle and then carried to the lodge arms extended with two hands gently supporting the folded flag from below. After some practice, this became a tradition for Paul and me. We even taught other kids the proper way to treat, fold and carry a flag.

Anti-American sentiment was not tolerated at the lodge. My parents were well aware that their summer livelihood depended on healthy US-Canadian relations and neither kid, employee, nor visitor was allowed to jeopardize this relationship.

I recall one example of this in the summer of 1976 just after the Montreal Canadiens won their 18th Stanley Cup. The Cup winner the previous two years was the Philadelphia Flyers, and, annually, we had a large group of obnoxious Flyers' fans from Philadelphia travel to the lodge.

In the summers of 1974 and 1975 these guests from Philadelphia would show up and gloat, with some good natured ribbing between them and my dad who adored his Montreal Canadiens and struggled with the idea of the Broad Street Bullies as Stanley Cup champions. But the exchanges were always genial and always between adults. The kids on either side of the debate remained silent. This silence was ominous.

I found the offspring of these Flyers' fans to be irritating and arrogant, much like the team itself. The "City of Brotherly Love" always struck me as a misnomer. These kids from Philadelphia knew my brother and I liked the Canadiens and behind the adults' backs the ribbing became more than good-natured. It was nasty at times, and it went both ways.

There was no way I was going to tolerate the bragging of these pushy kids from Philadelphia, especially when they not only promoted their own team and its successes but also when they openly mocked the Montreal Canadiens. I heard the French "frog" reference more than once. It didn't help that my Irish surname sounded French. Try explaining that to a pig-headed punk from Philly. For the sake of our livelihood, I could tolerate the personal attacks, but how dare they make fun of Guy Lafleur, Guy Lapointe, and others who wore the *bleu blanc et rouge.*

In response, Paul and I and others would return their taunts, openly criticizing the Flyers and some of their less skilled players, like Dave "the Hammer" Schultz who could fight but couldn't skate at all, same thing with Gary Dornhoefer and Bob "Hound Dog" Kelly. Don Saleski, one of the Flyers' role players, had a summer home in Newboro at the time, and we would ride our bikes by his house waiting to catch a glimpse of this NHL hockey player. I don't recall if we ever saw him. In my mind these guys were goons and didn't belong on the same ice as the Flying Frenchmen from Montreal.

One of the Philly boys and I were having a dispute about which hockey team was better. I can't remember the exact words we exchanged, but I do know we decided to have a fistfight to settle the issue. With the exception of a few brotherly spats, I had never been in a real fight in my life, let alone a bare knuckle fist fight. What was I thinking? I didn't know the first thing about fighting and cringed at the thought of hitting someone in the face with my fist or, even worse, getting hit in the face myself.

We agreed to the fight. We set the time and location. Greg, Steven, and Paul understood that I was in way over my head and decided I needed a crash course in fist fighting. The four of us went off to a secluded area to practice the art of fisticuffs. I think Steven consulted his brother Bruce for some technical advice. All I recall from the training session was Bruce's recommendation that I keep my thumbs outside of my enclosed fist or I could end up breaking my thumbs when I hit my opponent. Other than that I had no strategy, no confidence, no idea and worst of all no physical strength at the age of 11. I was a dead man. My only hope was that the fight would be called off or a boat would blow-up.

The other kid was the same age as me and roughly the same height. I felt nervous because of where he was from, not because of my parents "don't piss off the Americans" rule but because he was from the home of Rocky with a population of well over one million. Chances were good that he had been in many fights. I, on the other hand, was from Newboro population 310. The odds were against me.

We both showed up at the designated time and place for our *Rumble on the Rideau*. The catcalls, the innuendo, the bragging would all come to an end either way. There must have been a crowd of six or seven kids for the battle. The usual crew was in my corner (at least I assumed they were in my corner), and three or four friends supported Rocky Balboa.

The fight began before either of us was prepared. We were two feet apart and facing each other. I closed my eyes and started flailing away. He did the same, although I have no idea if his eyes were closed. The punches were flying both ways, but none were landing. His fist would meet my fist. His arm would hit my arm. Fist, arm, fist arm, left, right, left, right. We both failed to make any contact with either face or body. The farce went on for at least a minute, both of us punching wildly at the other but neither able to land one meaningful blow.

Finally, a disappointed spectator yelled, "Stop the fight. This isn't working. Neither one of you knows how to fight." Talk about stating the obvious.

The scrap was over, and we hadn't settled anything other than making it abundantly clear that neither one of us was a fighter. The brief exchange was embarrassing for both of us. The crowd dispersed, disappointment evident on their faces. After the fight, I couldn't face Paul, Steven, or Greg. I was hoping they would at least have one positive thing to say, but they didn't. They didn't say anything to make me feel better or to make me feel worse. They just walked away together—with me lagging behind them.

* * *

July 4th was still to come. This July 4th would be special because of the dual celebrations. The esteemed Newboro town council planned a day time parade and a fireworks extravaganza at the locks in the evening.

Parades have to be one of the more absurd human inventions, at least in small-town Canada. Get a group of people together, dress them up, position them on flatbed trucks, dress the truck up, throw in a couple clowns, a few animals, baton twirling, a fire truck or two or maybe even a tractor, some Shriners, the mayor, a marching band and voila—you have a ready-made parade. In small towns, the formula never changes.

There must have been eight or nine businesses in Newboro in the mid 1970s, three fishing lodges, some rental cottages, a general store, a pool hall/candy store, a tavern, a television repair shop, an antique store and a propane filling station. That's it. Regardless, even in the 1970s corporate participation was critical to a parade's success.

The pressure was on everyone to mount an unforgettable parade to celebrate the American and Newboro milestones. My parents felt the pressure more than others because their livelihood depended on American happiness. An underwhelming parade commemorating the birth of the most powerful nation on earth was not something they needed.

They took a lead role in parade planning, recruiting volunteers, soliciting support from local businesses, promoting the parade and even mapping the parade route, probably the most difficult task of all seeing that the main street through town doubled as County Road 42. In the summer this highway was busy. Even with the reduced speed limit signs on the outskirts of town, how could they possibly shut down the only link from the east to the Upper Rideau Lake in Westport at the height of tourist season? Parade organizers had to do some serious planning, and like most things in Newboro this planning was done hurriedly in the week leading up to the event.

The Poplars had to enter a float in the parade. This float had to not only capture the essence of the business but it had to somehow convey a clear link between Newboro's heritage and the bicentennial of America. No easy feat.

My parents decided a safe place to start was with flags, as my dad always was a bit of a collector. Apparently he knew a guy who knew a guy who made flags, so he special ordered some customized flags commemorating both birthdays.

The Newboro flag was a simple red and white design. Much smaller than the American flag, it was made of cheap, thin nylon. The American flag was made of a much thicker and better quality material. The design alteration to the American flag was significant with a large number 76 replacing the stars in the upper left corner. Thirteen embroidered stars encircled this number. It was an interesting modification to a powerful symbol. Hopefully, no one would be offended.

The Poplars' inner circle decided to enter an unseaworthy fishing guide boat. The vessel would sit on a boat trailer pulled by The Poplars' well-marked pickup truck. It was a marketing coup!

We had to transform the boat into the best float in the parade, keeping in mind that the competition was pretty thin. The cedar strip boat was in rough shape, and it needed a lot of work to look like more than just an old boat on a trailer being pulled by a truck. After some aggressive lobbying, our parents awarded Paul, Cathy and me the float decorating contract and provided us with reams of appropriately coloured streamers, tissue paper, ribbons and balloons.

Of course, the three of us had never decorated anything. At age three, my avant-garde sister decided to cover her bedroom walls with Vaseline. Yes, Vaseline. That was the closest any of us had come to actual decorating experience.

My parents enlisted an elderly couple from New Jersey, the Pucchios, to help us. They had been coming to the lodge every summer for decades, long before my parents took over the place. They were too old to handle a day of fishing. Most of the time they just sat around and visited with other guests, took in the scenery and dozed off in their Adirondack chairs. They were nice to Cathy, Paul, and me, which wasn't always the case with some of the old timers who just wanted to be left alone.

The Pucchios were patriotic Americans. They were old. Check that, they were ancient. Mr. Pucchio had served in the army during World War I. And they both knew a thing or two about parades and float decorating. What American doesn't? The foundation of their culture is the parade, any parade . . . celebratory or funereal, doesn't matter.

Louie delivered the porous cedar strip to the front lawn of our house, far away from the prying eyes of curious guests. The Pucchios arrived early on the morning of the 4th to help us decorate. They assumed they could just sit back and provide some gentle guidance from afar.

They soon witnessed the ineptitude of the Tallon children.

Paul wanted the red, white and blue ribbons to run in one direction, while Cathy wanted them to run in another. I wanted to emphasize the balloon motif. We weren't certain how to affix the decorations to the float so they would be secure. Scotch tape? Masking tape? Thumb tacks? We didn't know what we were doing, and the parade was scheduled to start in less than three hours.

Mercifully, the Pucchios took over the job of decorating the float, their initial hesitation to get involved replaced by nationalistic urgency. These two elderly people came to life, grabbing scissors, ribbon, and tape from our hands and designing their own parade float in the most patriotic manner possible. They couldn't use enough of the tri-coloured ribbon with the outside of the boat now invisible behind a sea of red, white and blue strands of tissue. And we needed to inflate the balloons. Paul and I were taking forever with this task. So the Pucchios took on this responsibility as well, more than once winding themselves so that they had to sit down to recover.

It was a hot July day, and these two elderly Americans were a marvel. We didn't mind, especially Paul and me. Our parents had selected us to ride on the float dressed as fishing guides. We were allowed to carry fishing rods as well and to cast out onto the road. Best of all, our father gave us the task of throwing candy at spectators along the parade route. This was what we were looking forward to most.

We finished decorating the float just in time. It looked splendid smothered under ribbons, flags and balloons, sort of like Charlie Brown's forlorn Christmas tree after Linus and his friends got a hold of it. The Pucchios, exhausted and on life support, stood back and admired their creation.

Paul and I agreed that it was the best float we had ever seen and that we would be proud to ride in it. Only later did we realize that there was nothing about the float that said *Happy Birthday Newboro*; it was an American theme from stem to stern. The much larger American flags and the reams of red, white and blue ribbon that draped the boat's façade overpowered the small Newboro centennial flags.

All that was left was for Paul and me to get in costume, and we would be off to the designated starting point for the parade. I should say I had to get in costume as Paul was already dressed as a fishing guide with his everyday attire of jeans, flannel shirt and fishing cap. Roughly the same size as Paul, all I had to do was search his dresser and grab his back-up fishing guide outfit.

The parade route ran along the outer streets of the town first and then cut down Drummond Street/County Road 42 for the grand finale. There must have been three or four floats (and I use that word loosely), a fire truck, a propane truck, and a couple vintage tractors—a total of ten entries maybe.

On the outer circuit of the parade attendance was sparse, with the odd person standing in front of his house talking to someone and then turning around and noticing the approaching spectacle. I am not sure how well the parade was advertised, but many people seemed to be caught off guard by it. Paul and I were free to cast away along the side of the road for the first part of the parade. Only once did Paul cast too far and get his hook with a plastic fish on it caught in road-side bushes. The entire parade had to stop as my dad climbed out of the truck and unhooked the snagged fishing line.

The parade continued, and we rounded the corner and headed towards Drummond Street. We realized that we still had a heap of candy remaining. At best, we had counted ten spectators along the parade route. But that's the magic of a small town parade. The streets should be deserted because everyone in the town is participating in the parade.

By small town standards, Drummond Street was packed, however. They must have bussed spectators in from out of town because there were at least 150 onlookers lining the street. They were all squinting in the direction of the approaching procession.

Paul and I were in our element. We were waving flags, smiling ear to ear while throwing candy in all directions. The sun was shining, people were ecstatic, flashbulbs exploded. It was perfect. Then we saw Steven and knew that we had to fulfill our part of our pre-arranged deal with him. I am not certain what his part of the deal was.

Steven found out that we would be giving away candy along the parade route, and he reminded Paul and me of the importance of his friendship. He demanded that we give him as much candy as we could when we saw him in the crowd. Contractually obligated and with an excess of candy, we showered him with most of the candy we had remaining in the boat.

This was no gentle candy shower; it was more like a torrential downpour. Steven and those around him couldn't have been happier, except for the elderly woman who Paul hit in the eye with an errant caramel. At least I think it was Paul.

As we passed the remnants of the jubilant crowd and headed for home, Paul and I realized that we had just been part of something monumental, an event much bigger than the two of us. We agreed that everything had gone splendidly and that we should do it again next year.

But this parade would be Newboro's last.

That Smell

Community celebrations in Newboro were infrequent but memorable. Two such events that stand out in addition to the Centennial Parade in 1976 were Newboro's one and only rock concert and the annual summer carnival at the locks.

A town with a population of 310 had little drawing power for the popular musical acts of the day. Not surprisingly, The Eagles, Nazareth, Alice Cooper and others bypassed Newboro on their cross Canada summer tours in the 1970s. The best teenagers and music fans could do was to travel to Ottawa, Toronto or Montreal to see the larger acts or to Kingston to see smaller acts. This was one of the sacrifices one made when living in a small town where radio and two television channels represented the only connections to the outside world.

In the summer of 1977, the local council decided to invite a rock band to Newboro to perform at the town hall, seating capacity 100. Even more surprising was that the local municipal government was able to convince a band, any band, to come to Newboro in the middle of summer. All that remained was the marketing campaign.

The band was obscure, very obscure. Their name was Midway. We found this out from the promotional posters hanging on every telephone pole in town. We had a couple concert posters in the main lodge, although the clientele at The Poplars was from the Eisenhower era and couldn't have cared less about a hippy rock band.

As depicted on the posters, the band members looked very much like the members of the Scottish band Nazareth. They had long scraggly hair, goatees and that emaciated rock star look that was popular in the 1970s. The posters claimed that they were an "up and coming band" from somewhere near Toronto.

The obvious question was, if they were up and coming why were they playing Newboro? Did someone have dirt on one of the band members? Up and coming bands do not play towns the size of Newboro. A more likely scenario was that they were on their way down. It was the late 70s and disco was all the rage. And punk music from England and New York City had overtaken the classic rock genre.

The build up to the concert was impressive despite the musical winds of change at the time. Newboro was at least five years behind the times, so booking a hard rock outfit like Midway made sense. The teenagers and young adults in the town didn't have a great deal to keep themselves busy even during the summer months. Hanging out at Vic's pool hall or traveling to nearby towns were the main pastimes for anyone over 14. For these small-town youths this rock concert was going to be the best part of their summer regardless of how substandard the band may be. It was the talk of the town for weeks leading up to the early August concert.

My sister was 16 years old in the summer of 1977. There was no way she and her friends were going to miss out on the only rock band to ever play Newboro. She even had a couple friends coming in from out of town, so in their world this was going to be significant.

My brother and I wanted to go to the concert too. The posters were everywhere, and we were curious. Plus, we had access to our sister's record collection. Whether Midway sounded like these musicians didn't matter to us. We asked our parents more than once if we could attend the concert. Each time their united response was the same: "You boys are too young for that sort of thing."

What does "that sort of thing" mean? Could they have been any more ambiguous? What did they know about "that sort of thing" anyway? They listened to Tommy Dorsey and Glen Miller big band music. We were more familiar with "that sort of thing" than they were. But they put braces on our teeth and food on the table, so we were in no position to question their authority. The best we could negotiate was a ride in the back of the station wagon when my mom drove Cathy and her friends to the concert. The venue was a mere ten minute walk from our home, but my mother needed to satisfy her own curiosity about Cathy's rock and roll lifestyle.

The night of the concert, the streets of Newboro resembled a pilgrimage. There were teenagers everywhere walking in the direction of the community hall. They were drinking, they were smoking, they were listening to music in cars. They were celebrating. Cars lined both sides of the narrow streets for blocks in all directions. At the site of the concert, traffic was at a standstill. A standstill in Newboro—that was a first.

With my brother and me awestruck in the back of the wagon and my sister and her friends in the seat in front of us, my mother approached the scene, her eyes wide and the speedometer barely moving. We were traveling so slow that everything around us moved in super slow motion. Who were these concert goers? Newboro had 25 teenagers tops, so most of these faces were unfamiliar to us. They all looked the same too, just like the band members on the promo posters. It was like Woodstock—Newboro edition. Peace Love and Music. Alcohol, drugs, and sex too.

We arrived at the town hall, which was constructed in 1840 and had served as Newboro's court house for many years. My mother pulled off to the side of the street to allow another car to pass. She read my sister the usual list of rules: no drinking, no smoking, no drugs, no funny business . . . and, of course, my sister nodded her head in agreement. What else was she going to do, tell the truth? Cathy and her friends got out of the wagon, but so did my mom. Ouch! That must have been a major blow to Cathy's teenage ego—walking into a rock concert with her mother at her side. Of course, Paul and I couldn't sit in the car unattended with all the crazies about, so we jumped out and followed them to the front entrance of the hall.

Cathy was not pleased. Her mom and little brothers were tagging along. How embarrassing! We followed her right to the front door. The band had begun their first set, and their music was deafening—so loud that I couldn't distinguish one instrument from another let alone hear a singer. The stage was aglow with band members silhouetted against a misty, purple backdrop. As my sister entered the darkened hall, Paul and I peered beyond her.

"This doesn't look like the town hall," I mused.

In front of the illuminated stage, the room was dark and packed as far as we could tell. Strange odours emanated from the crowd.

"What's that smell?" Paul asked my mother.

She shook her head in disgust. Before she could do or say anything else, Cathy and her friends vanished into the mass of sweaty humanity that filled the hall.

My mother grabbed Paul and me by our wrists and dragged us back to the car. We jumped in the backseat, and my mother took her position behind the steering wheel. We didn't move. My mom just sat there staring at the hall and watching the hordes of teenagers coming and going from the venue. She was not pleased, but there was nothing she could do.

She shifted the car into drive and prepared to pull back on to the street. But she was blocked in at the front, so she had to back up to get around the car in front. Twilight faded. There was limited visibility around the car. Plus, there were people everywhere, and my mother was agitated. She backed up but didn't check the space behind her. Before we could warn her, my mother backed right into the ditch that ran parallel to the street.

Crunch! is all I remember hearing as the backend of the car hit the ditch.

This wasn't some wussy city ditch. This was the real thing—a three foot drop off into a gully. A culvert I think it is called. The front end of the wagon was suspended in air, and Paul and I were staring up at the night sky. My mother put the car in drive and hit the accelerator. The engine revved, but we didn't move. She got out, jumped out to be precise, and surveyed the damage. Of course, we followed.

The back end of the station wagon was deep in the ditch. There was no way the car was going to move without divine intervention or a tow truck.

"Dad isn't going to like this," I said.
"Your father doesn't have to know about this, Jimmy!" was her prompt reply.
"Oh yes he does," I quipped.
"Jimmy, that's enough!"

My mom had a line. It was a flexible line. But when someone crossed her line, that was it.

A crowd of teenagers surrounded the car; some we recognized, but most we didn't. My mother told Paul and me to get back in the car.

"Why?" Paul asked.

The look from my mother didn't allow for a follow-up question. We climbed into the car. My mom continued to survey the situation. Then we saw her talking to someone behind the car. Before we knew it she was getting into the car.

"Hold on, boys," is all she said as a group of five or six large teenage boys took position at the back end of the car.

Someone tapped on the roof of the car. My mom hit the gas. The station wagon moved maybe a foot. Another tap, more gas and the car moved another foot. After the third tap and more gas, the car lurched out of the ditch and came to a stop on the street. The crowd of teenagers around the car let out a cheer. My mother sighed. She was famous for her sighs. She rolled down her window and thanked the pushers (get it?), and we were on our way. My mother was no longer agitated about the company my sister was keeping that night at the Midway concert.

* * *

The annual summer carnival never changed while we lived in Newboro. It took place the third week of July, and the itinerary included speed boat races throughout the day, children's games at the locks in the afternoon, bingo and roulette later in the evening, a chicken barbecue for 100s of tourists and residents, and a dance with recorded or live music, usually country and western. The evening concluded with an impressive fireworks display over the lake. This was the successful formula every summer.

Because it never changed the annual summer carnival was the perfect celebration for a child. Every summer we were neither surprised nor disappointed.

This was a small-town fair. The quality control—or quality for that matter—was not always what it should have been. The organizers used the same games of chance from the carnival's inception, some 15 years earlier. The games were sketchy at best, but it wasn't so much the games that we were concerned about. We were more interested in the prizes.

Because carnival organizers used the same skill-testing games each summer, we improved our performance every year. The carnival games were simple and traditional: balloons and darts, the fish tank, a kids' roulette wheel, and some sort of squirt gun and target exercise. Nothing spectacular, but nothing we couldn't dominate either.

The fish tank was an antique floor model Coca Cola machine filled with water and semi-submerged toy fish. On the underside of each fish was the name of a corresponding prize—something cheap, plastic and useful for about five minutes.

The water in the tank was murky, a bit rusty too, so the game wasn't as easy as it looked. The volunteer carnie provided us with a fishing line and hook attached to a small stick. It turned out to be an exercise in luck more than anything as the day progressed and the discolouration of the water increased. We always caught a fish or two, and the two minute time limit was flexible. We paid the 25 cent entry fee only once, so we always came out ahead. The prizes were underwhelming, but their cumulative value far exceeded a quarter.

At supper time we returned to the lodge for dinner as it was only a couple minutes from the locks, and our mother expected us to check in with her at least once during the day. One summer, however, when we were under Cathy's supervision our parents gave us permission to stay at the carnival throughout the afternoon and evening without returning to the lodge for dinner. This meant we would be able to experience some of the delicious food the carnival offered up to the masses in the tented area near the lockmaster's quarters.

The food looked and smelled wonderful. Corn on the cob, barbecued chicken, potato salad, and a collection of fruit pies. Volunteers from the community prepared most of the food on site. We assumed all of it was fresh and healthy, not like the cuisine at traveling fairs and carnivals.

I recall my sister rounding up Paul and me, and the three of us heading to the food tent to get a plate of this legendary cuisine. It tasted fantastic. The three of us were content as we devoured our meals and sipped lemonade while sitting in the open air tent overlooking the lake.

My parents were obsessed with properly cooked poultry. My worry wart mother's background in public health was an important part of this. Call it paranoia, call it caution, but they rarely served chicken at the lodge because of all the meats it was the one most likely to carry some sort of bacteria that, even when cooked thoroughly, could be passed on to the guests. The last thing they wanted was one of the guests complaining about food poisoning at The Poplars.

As a result, the opportunity to eat barbecued chicken was rare, so we seized any chance we could. After eating everything on our plates, we were ready to go for the evening as the games continued. Best of all, the fireworks were still to come. When we finally arrived home after 10 PM, we were exhausted but ecstatic about our day at the carnival.

Time passed, perhaps a couple days, and I started feeling different. It was the middle of summer, and usually at this time I was in peak kid condition. This was the pre-Nintendo era, so most kids couldn't help but be fit, especially in the summer. Something was wrong, however. I had no energy. I felt light headed and fuzzy. My stomach was churning. I didn't feel like doing anything. All of these symptoms hit me at once one sunny day in late July. I mentioned my condition to my mom. She said I was likely coming down with "something".

By late afternoon, I was feeling sicker than I could ever remember. I was lethargic. I recall that I was sitting on the back step of the storage shed. My head was spinning. My stomach was aching. I also remember detecting a strange, sweet smell, an aroma that I had never experienced before. I couldn't decide if it was a good smell or a bad smell, a food smell or a different kind of smell altogether. When I put my arm up to my nose, the odour became stronger.

This is strange, I thought. *Why does my arm have this unusual sweet smell to it?* I lifted my other arm. It smelled funny too.

All I could smell was the unusual sweet odour, and it was making me even more nauseous. It overpowered every other aroma, including the pleasant ones drifting out of the lodge kitchen.

Soon the aching in my stomach became more intense. I forgot about the smell. I made a mad dash to the house and the bathroom where I spent a good part of the evening and the next couple days. Finally, my parents realized that something wasn't right, and I received the medical attention I required.

As it turned out, my sister Cathy was not well either. She had spent much of her day in the bathroom. She was not playing amateur cosmetician either. When I got up to the house that day, she was lying on her bed looking gravely ill.

The next day after some blood tests in Kingston, doctors diagnosed us with something called Salmonella, an acute intestinal infection transmitted to humans by eating foods contaminated with animal feces. Animal feces! Some American scientist named Salmon discovered the virus in the early part of the 20th century. The most common carrier of this virus is poultry, especially poorly prepared or under cooked poultry.

My parents' greatest fear had been realized. But it was not the infection of their guests; it was the infection of their own kids. My brother Paul did not get sick. He ate the same food we did but didn't display any of the symptoms of Salmonella. But Cathy and I had all the symptoms: diarrhea, fever, nausea, dizziness and abdominal cramps, and that saccharine aroma seeping from our pores. It wouldn't go away.

The doctor informed us that the illness usually lasted four to seven days. The only thing we could do was stay comfortable, stay hydrated and wait for the symptoms to pass. The diarrhea was the most significant problem as Cathy and I were vying for the use of our only bathroom. After a couple more days, I started to feel better. Cathy didn't. The doctor in Kingston informed us that Salmonella can affect people differently with some experiencing more serious symptoms than others. In cases of severe diarrhea hospitalization might have to occur.

Cathy was admitted to hospital in Kingston. The doctor coolly informed my parents that if Salmonella gets into the bloodstream it can be life threatening, just what they needed to hear. She spent a week in the hospital on antibiotics and hooked up to an IV. My symptoms disappeared altogether by day five. Cathy was better by day ten. Even now, I can still recall the sweet smell of the Salmonella bug.

The barbecued chicken at the summer carnival was the culprit. Volunteers prepared it in an open-air, make-shift kitchen in the middle of summer. We had no idea how many others became ill, but no one else complained. Most likely those who were sick thought it was a bad case of stomach flu. As for my parents, their fear of poultry intensified. Their kids bought into their paranoia, no longer requesting barbecued chicken on the menu at the lodge and overcooking chicken well into their adult lives.

Here's Johnny!

Every summer for five days in July, The Poplars Resort transformed into a three-ring circus. Not the kind with medicated animals and frantic midgets, but the other kind of circus. The sort of circus that when it ended, left those who had witnessed it feeling bewildered. These five days in July impacted anyone connected to the lodge. And the memories lingered.

Cartoonist Johnny Hart and his entourage of 10-12 cartoonists and illustrators started vacationing at The Poplars in 1969, and turned the resort into party central. Sometimes showing up in cars, sometimes in a Winnebago, sometimes in a bus, these artists, performers and PR men would drive up from Endicott, New York with the sole intention of having a better time than the previous summer. Alcohol was the catalyst, of course. Any plans the other guests had for a peaceful week at the lodge would come to an end.

One by one they would file out of the Winnebago, beer in one hand and Crown Royal in the other. If I were to play a word association game today and had to respond to the words "stubby beer bottle" I would answer Johnny Hart. I had never seen that many stacked cases of beer before. Because the lodge didn't have a liquor licence, the guests were responsible for supplying their own booze. Johnny Hart and his fellow revellers brought enough booze to supply the town of Newboro, population 310. The oddest thing about their arrival was that rarely, if ever, did I see anyone with luggage other than the blue velvet Crown Royal bags and cases of beer.

Their ringleader was Johnny Hart, the quietest of the bunch as is often the case with ringleaders. His cartoons *The Wizard of Id* and *B.C.* were popular then and syndicated all over the world. He produced these comic strips right up to his death in 2007. I didn't understand many of his comic strips at the time and asked my parents to explain them to me. After their explanations, I was still left scratching my head. I suppose the depth of meaning of his cartoons and their social commentary exceeded the capabilities of a child's mind. His drawings were fantastic, however, especially the bizarre pre-historic cavemen figures of the *B.C.* comic strip.

Johnny's group took over an entire guest house, usually Broderick House, which was more like a home that slept up to twelve people than it was a guest house. This house became the command centre for their vacation. In the summer of 76, they took over our house, too. We had to stay at our neighbour's house. This was a first for us and gave us kids a clear message: We all had to sacrifice for the business.

Vacation is an odd word to use to describe the five days these merry men (there were never any women, excluding the buxom lodge waitresses of course) spent at the lodge. I think celebration is more apropos. A couple weeks before their arrival, Johnny would send the itinerary for the week to my parents. This was no routine itinerary of arrival and departure times; this was a day-to-day breakdown of the week's activities built around their annual fishing derby known as the *Clumsy Carp Open*. The illustrations and text for the itinerary were hand drawn and printed by Johnny himself. The cover featured a caricature of fellow cartoonist Jack Caprio under water and about to swallow a fish.

In 1976, the visit I remember best, Johnny Hart and his crew were celebrating *The 7th Annual Bicentennial Clumsy Carp Open*, from July 5th to the 9th. Everyone expected this event to be the greatest extravaganza of them all. The itinerary for the week was as follows:

Monday	**July 5th**	**Depart at 7 AM, arrive Poplars and Fish**
Tuesday	**July 6th**	**Speidi Roast**
Wednesday	**July 7th**	**Horseshoe and Hole-in-One Contest** (casting tournament, not golf)
Thursday	**July 8th**	**Fish Fry and Awards Dinner**
Friday	**July 9th**	**Fish and Split**

Poster for 7th Annual Bicentennial Clumsy Carp Open

Modelled after the *Dean Martin Celebrity Roasts* of the 1960s, the "Speidi Roast" skewered a different member of Johnny's entourage each summer. My brother and I were not permitted to attend these roasts as our parents classified them as R-rated. I'm not sure I would have understood the jokes anyway, unless I brought Dougie McViety along to explain them. Lying in bed, Paul and I could hear howls of laughter wafting up from the main lodge dining room. The roars went on for a couple hours.

The alcohol fuelled week-long competition culminated in Awards Night the evening before they departed. On this special night, Johnny and members of his entourage showed up in their finest formal wear, so they must have brought clothing after all. The grand prize was *The Ultimate Clumsy Carp One of a Kind Prestige Trophy*. Johnny presented this award to the fisherman with the greatest accumulation of tonnage for all fish caught between the 5th and 6 PM on the 8th. Someone in the group maintained a log book to ensure that all contestants were honest about their daily catches. Each entry had to be attested by another member of the group. There was prize money too. Ten dollars was awarded each day to the individual who caught the "heaviest single fish of any species". As Johnny Hart explained, if the fish was married it couldn't be counted in the competition.

The festive mood overflowed to the rest of the lodge. By mid-week guests and staff members, including my parents, were involved in the madness. That was the first time I ever saw my mother drunk, I mean totally soused. Not a pretty sight or fond memory.

On the final night of their stay after the awards' gala, Johnny and some of his cartoonists set up shop in the games room and drew personalized cartoons for some of the guests and staff. Johnny created cartoons depicting my mom and dad, Cathy, Paul and me doing various crazy things around the lodge. Johnny signed these cartoons for each one of us. I still have many of these cartoons today. Because of his generosity towards my family, we all thought of Johnny Hart as Robin Hood, and the rest of his crew as the Merrymen.

* * *

In 1976, my parents decided to add a second cookout the Thursday night of Johnny Hart's stay. Throughout the summer, this cookout was reserved for Saturday nights, but the rarely used "celebrity exception clause" kicked in for Johnny Hart.

The usual preparation and set up took place. Busboys hauled dining room tables and chairs to the lawn in front of the main lodge. Dining room staff lined up food serving tables in front of the main walkway. Red and white checkered table cloths covered each table. It was an idyllic image with the setting sun and shimmering lake in the background. Everyone was in the mood for a celebration, some more than others. Some patrons hid pitchers of bourbon and lemonade under their tables for easy access. The weather cooperated. There were no exploding boats. My parents were more relaxed than usual.

The kitchen staff served the food, and the guests, including the cartoonists, enjoyed the finest offerings from the lodge kitchen. Hot dogs, hamburgers, tomato aspic (a side dish name that still makes me laugh), various noodle and potato salads, iced tea, lemonade, assorted pies, chocolate mousse, jello topped with whipped crème. The menu was traditional, but the guests didn't want it any other way. Nearing the end of the meal as the guests, probably close to 70, were enjoying some coffee and dessert something unexpected happened.

Of course, Paul and I had a front row seat for this event as if we were anticipating more unexpected hijinx. It was the lodge, the 1970s; something was bound to happen.

We were sitting in our traditional positions on the edge of the sidewalk inhaling our desserts when we heard gasps and shrieks coming from some of the guests sitting nearer to the waterfront. Soon there was a cascade of screams, louder this time and primarily from the older women in the crowd.

Paul and I couldn't see anything. We stood up. We still couldn't see anything. We didn't know where to look. It sounded like the commotion was down by the water, near Ward Hall. Some guests stood; some remained seated. Some laughed. Some pointed. Others covered their eyes. Others were expressionless.

Within seconds we discovered what all the fuss was: Two grown men, stark naked, darted through the crowd swerving right by the serving tables and the shocked staff, right by my battle-hardened parents, and right past my brother and me as we sat there, our mouths open wide and full of chocolate mousse. The runners raced up the hill to Broderick House.

It happened so fast that no one knew what to make of it. The gasps and shrieks gave way to an eerie silence as people began to digest the spectacle. Then pockets of laughter rose up from the guest tables. My mortified mother and stoic father began to laugh.

Paul and I were dumbfounded. Why had these two naked men just run past us? Were they being chased? Had someone stolen their clothes? Killer bees? Was it killer bees from Africa, and if so why were these men naked? We didn't have any answers.

Later we discovered that what these two men did during the cookout was called "streaking". It was a popular activity all over the world at that time, especially at sporting events, such as European soccer games and retirement home lawn bowling tournaments in Miami. It was, as our parents explained to us, some individuals' idea of a silly prank and a great way to receive some attention.

While some of the elderly guests took offence at the display of flesh, the majority appreciated the absurdity of the moment and seemed glad to be witnesses to the show. The streakers turned out to be two young apprentice cartoonists who were travelling with Johnny Hart. No one really knew for sure if it was their own idea or part of an elaborate initiation ritual among cartoonists. Paul and I had witnessed our first naked grown-ups. It was an image that neither one of us would get out of our head for some time.

* * *

Weeks later and inspired by the events on that July evening, Paul, Steven and I took our bikes down the graveyard road. We dismounted in a secluded area that contained five or six private cottages. We decided we would try streaking just like the two men did on the front lawn of the lodge. The only difference was that there was no one, at least we saw no one, outside that afternoon to witness our outlandish behaviour. And we decided, in a moment of shame, to keep our underwear on when we ran around these empty cottages. It was over in less than a minute, and it lacked the dramatic impact of the real thing. As we got dressed, we were all quite embarrassed about our pathetic attempt at streaking. We agreed to never speak of it again.

The Russian and the Dwarf

On the occasion of my mother's 40th birthday my father decided to do something special. He always had a flare for the dramatic. His theatrical moments included attending antique auctions with my mother. My mom was the antique expert in the family, but on impulse my dad would start bidding on a piece, usually a valuable piece. He wouldn't stop bidding until the item was his. This behaviour was out of character for my dad. He was a frugal fellow, likely because he was the keeper of the books at The Poplars.

The celebration of my mother's 40th birthday in 1971 was to be no small affair. My dad decided to recruit a Russian artist to paint a portrait of my mother. The Russian part mattered less than the price tag, I think, although my father had a thing for foreigners. He once hired an alcoholic chef from France after the lodge's regular cook walked out in a huff one day. On paper, this French chef had all the credentials; however, he was a drunk. Worst of all, he had no idea what he was doing in the kitchen. Nor did he understand the traditional cuisine of a fishing lodge in rural Ontario. His dishes were indescribable and inedible. He lasted three days.

The Russian artist had recently immigrated to Canada. His English was not the best. My dad arranged for the portrait to be started and completed in the summer months, not in the winter, even though my mother's birthday is February 6th.

When this flamboyant artist showed up in the middle of August, there was no way my mother would have time to sit for hours at a time over a two week period. The lodge would fall apart.

My dad insisted. The artist was adamant that he needed my mother's undivided attention. The daily sittings, despite my mother's protests, began in August of 1971.

The artist chose a remote country road on the edge of town for the backdrop of the portrait. He reminded my parents that portrait painting was serious business for both artist and subject. Apparently, he had a reputation to uphold. A reputation for what, no one knew for sure.

The early stages of the process were not successful. My mother and Ivan were at odds. He demanded that she relax. She refused to cooperate.

The painter: "Joan, you must remove vorry from your face."
My mother: "Why? It is my best feature."

The artist persisted. His solution was ingenious. Ivan decided that the remedy for the tension was simple: vodka. Or as Ivan pronounced it: "wodka". He possessed an ample supply of his favourite Russian spirit.

To get her to relax, he kept feeding her glass after glass of vodka. Soon the tension in her face disappeared. With an inebriated subject, the artist was able to get down to painting the portrait.

Weeks later, after some additional touch up work by the artist, the portrait was officially unveiled. My father presented it to my mother. He loved it; she hated it. He wanted it to hang in the living room; she wanted to burn it. They compromised on the family room, the dimly lit corner.

Today, I am the proud keeper of this portrait of my mother at 40. I think it is a fine work and it certainly captures her natural beauty. However, if one examines the portrait closely looking at her eyes and her mouth, the discerning eye can see that she is three sheets to the wind.

Joan Tallon, August 1971

* * *

I have had a life-long fascination with midgets and, by extension, dwarves. At the lodge I often saw a person who had all the characteristics of a grown man, yet he was roughly the same height as I was. He was bow-legged and his head over-sized (dead giveaways for dwarfism). Other than these characteristics, he looked like an unusually short man. Paul and I were wary of him.

His name was Jimmy Houghton. He used to be a professional wrestler and, rumour had it, a very good one. His arms and legs though short were massive. He was clearly a man of great strength. Jimmy had given up the rigours of professional wrestling and decided to move to the country to simplify his life. Perhaps he and my dad had more in common than they realized with their mutual desire for simplicity. Jimmy was married and had three kids, two sons and a daughter. I remember being confused by the appearance of his family.

His wife was a tall, slim, and graceful woman. His daughter shared these traits. His sons, however, looked just like Jimmy only younger. I was reluctant to ask anyone to explain this to me. I just kept my mouth shut and wondered the same thing every time I saw Jimmy with his family. Paul and I kept our distance.

At the lodge, Jimmy worked as a fishing guide, one of many such guides who took guests out in their guide boat and led them to some of the prime fishing spots on the lake. The guide would do everything for the guest with the exception of actually catching fish. Sometimes they would have to do that too.

Some guides were legendary on Newboro Lake. Art Pritchard and his son Tommy were the best. If *TripAdvisor.com* existed back then, they would have been ranked one and two respectively for Newboro Lake fishing guides. Their services were in demand. As a result, they would be on the lake daily throughout the summer. Jimmy, however, was not in demand. His *TripAdvisor* rating would have been much lower. He was legendary for other reasons, however.

Jimmy Houghton was the friendliest man you would ever meet—when he wasn't drinking. Alcohol changed him. He became aggressive, angry and foul mouthed. And there is nothing more frightening than a drunken midget, I mean dwarf, with a hot temper. My father took the guests going to Jimmy's boat aside and instructed them not to give Jimmy any alcohol while they were out on the lake. Not even a beer. One drink, he informed them, would lead to a desire for another, and by then it would be too late. The outcome could prove deadly, especially since Jimmy was the person steering the boat.

Most guests adhered to this and abstained from alcohol while fishing with Jimmy. This was disheartening for many guests because the highlight of a day with a fishing guide was the shore dinner. The temptation to drink during these cookouts was difficult for many to resist. Often a plan for a full day of fishing would freefall into an afternoon of drunken debauchery. This is what happened to Jimmy Houghton one day when his fishing guests failed to heed my dad's warning.

It was early evening when an obviously drunk Jimmy Houghton returned to the lodge with his drunken guests in tow. Jimmy slammed his custom guide boat into the dock. It was evident to everyone that he was hammered. With assistance from an amused but concerned guest, Jimmy managed to climb out of the boat and stagger along the dock towards shore. He came close to falling in the lake on this relatively short journey. He was in a foul mood, cursing everyone and everything in his path. It was a pathetic sight. It might have been funny for some, but I don't recall anyone laughing. My brother and I ran for cover behind a poplar tree.

Jimmy staggered up to the lodge and into the kitchen via the back entrance. My mother often worked late into the evening in the kitchen, making sure everything was ready for the following day. She was the second cook at the lodge, and she was called in as relief many times.

Jimmy saw my mom alone and working away in the kitchen. The kitchen was a large space with walls of shelving, a walk-in refrigerator, freezers, a bank of ovens and burners, and ample space for dishwashing. In the centre of the kitchen was a rectangular stainless steel food preparation island over ten feet long and three feet wide.

My mom was an attractive woman in her prime. A short but discerning individual, Jimmy noticed this. On this night, he discovered that she was alone in the kitchen.

Fuelled by alcohol, Jimmy approached my mom in a lustful manner. She knew of Jimmy's reputation. She smelled alcohol. She backed away and headed in the opposite direction. Jimmy followed. What was at first a hurried pace for my mom became a frantic sprint. Jimmy chased her around the food prep table. Eventually—apparently retired midget wrestlers are faster than middle-aged women—he caught her.

My mother turned to face Jimmy, perhaps deciding to confront him rather than continue the absurd chase. Jimmy reached out and up. He wrapped his arms around my mother's waist and gave her a bear hug.

"Get your hands off me, little man!" my mother shouted.

She proceeded to strike Jimmy over the head with a pot. Jimmy let go. My mother fled to the safety of the social area of the main lodge where guests were watching TV and playing cards. Jimmy disappeared. He didn't reappear for weeks. His employment at the lodge was infrequent after the encounter with my mother. I am not certain where my dad was during all this. I am not certain if there was any additional fallout from the incident. I do know, however, that my fascination with midgets can be traced back to Jimmy Houghton.

Das Boot—Part II

You'd poison a blind man's dog and steal his cane.
You'd gift wrap a leper and mail it to your Aunt Jane
Oh you can go to hell . . .
You're something that never should have happened
You'd even make your grandma sick.

—Alice Cooper ("Go to Hell",
Alice Cooper Goes to Hell, 1976)

I was six years old when I pooed in my sister's boot. Her boots were brand new, those knee-high shiny white go-go boots with heels popular in the 1960s. Think of Nancy Sinatra's footwear in her video for her song "These Boots Were Made for Walking" and you get the idea. These boots were made for something else, as well.

In 1971 my sister was ten years old. She was someone I looked up to. She was smart, funny and always busy doing something interesting. She had lots of friends even at a young age. Her trademark was her infectious full body giggle. She used to start slowly and then pick up momentum if something struck her as humorous. The giggle took over her entire body and concluded with her hugging herself to get it under control. By this time we'd all be laughing, not because of a joke or something particularly funny, but because of Cathy's outrageous giggle.

She made all of us laugh, all the time. She looked out for Paul and me and was often our advocate in many a messy situation where we faced inevitable doom for having done something to piss off our parents or a babysitter. There was nothing to dislike about Cathy.

In the early spring of 1971, a full six months before Led Zeppelin *IV* hit the record stores, "the incident" occurred. I had no reason to harbour any ill feelings for Cathy. She had never ever done anything to harm me or to get me in trouble. We enjoyed each other's company, but also knew when to give each other some space, the perfect sibling relationship.

She had a friend visiting, as usual. Like most young girls, they were into dressing up, putting on makeup, and doing their hair. The bathroom was their salon. We had one bathroom in the house, so we knew that if Cathy had a friend coming over we had better plan our bathroom visits accordingly.

She was in the bathroom with Pamela Stuffles (one of the best surnames ever). They were applying makeup. They were reapplying makeup, then doing their hair and redoing their hair. They were in there for the long haul. Perhaps we should have held the architect of the house accountable for this serious design flaw. Rumour was that our house had been converted from a carriage house for horses back in the early 1900s, so we were lucky to have one bathroom. Essentially, Paul, Cathy and I *were* raised in barn.

When the urge hit, Cathy and her friend represented my only barrier to relief. I knocked on the door. No response. I knocked on the door again. Nothing . . . except muffled giggles.

"Cathy, I have to go. Let me in please," I begged.
"Go away. We are busy."
"Cathy, I really have to go!"
"Go away! We're almost finished."

I walked away despondent and descended the stairs. I had to go somewhere. I was desperate. I needed privacy, but comfort and convenience were important as well. After a quick search of the house—why going outside didn't occur to me I don't know—I decided that the walk-in closet in the front hallway was the ideal location. I could close the door, take care of matters and no one would know the difference. It never occurred to me that I should destroy the evidence.

I snuck into the front closet and shut the door behind me. It was peaceful in the closet. There was some light shining through under the door. I felt around for anything still not certain of my receptacle of choice and came upon something that was knee high on me with an opening at the top. It was one of Cathy's white go-go boots. Perfect! I would worry about the consequences later . . .

I decided to hide out in my bedroom. I did not want to talk to anyone. I tried to reassure myself that everything was going to be okay. Someone, somewhere must have defecated in a go-go boot at some point. I was no trend-setter, even back then. I heard Cathy and Pamela come out of the bathroom and sneak downstairs. They were still giggling.

Maybe she won't wear her go-go boots, I thought. She had more practical footwear options. She didn't have to make a fashion statement every time she left the house. I heard the front door open and close. All was quiet in the house. Cathy was walking Pamela home.

I tip-toed downstairs and peeked into the front closet. Cathy's white go-go boots were gone! Why hadn't she said anything? Why hadn't I heard her screams of disgust? Why was I still alive? What is the meaning of life? Okay, that last question didn't occur to me until much later in my childhood, during the Carter administration in the late 70s.

All I could do was wait. I had never faced the wrath of Cathy before. I didn't even know if she had wrath. I was worried and started to regret my desperate act. Then it occurred to me: Blame Paul. It worked most other times. Paul never seemed to mind. In fact, I think he liked the attention.

Shortly after leaving the house, my sister came storming through the front door crying.

"Someone pooed in my boot!" she cried.
I was shocked.
Who would do such a thing? I wondered.
I ran to console her.

"Cathy, what's the matter?" I said in my most empathetic manner.
"Look . . ." she said pulling her foot out of her boot.
"Yuck!" I exclaimed. "That's gross."

Cathy was upset, more upset than I had ever witnessed before. Still sobbing, she sat down on the bottom step of the stairs and gingerly began to take her sock off. Hearing the commotion, my parents finally decided to investigate.

Sure, I thought, *NOW they show up. Where were they 45 minutes ago?*

The inquiry into the shit-in-the-boot affair was officially underway. It was a kangaroo court: Names were mentioned, fingers were pointed, and Paul was targeted.

"Who would do such a thing?" my mother repeated.
"Maybe, Paul. He is pretty young and only recently potty trained, you know," I offered.

But no one was buying it. All evidence was starting to point to me. Cathy explained what had gone on in the bathroom and how I had knocked on the door and then disappeared when she (allegedly) opened it.

Okay, the jig is up, I thought.

With everyone looking at me, I had to admit guilt, the most humiliating moment of my life—ever.

With my head hanging low all I could say was, "Okay, I did it."
"Jimmy!" they all gasped.
"But," I countered, "Cathy wouldn't let me in the bathroom!"

All eyes shifted to Cathy.

"Cathy, is this true?" my mother asked.
Cathy, her head hanging down, replied quietly, "Yes, it's true."
"Cathy!" my mother gasped. "How could you? You know we only have one bathroom in the house."

Aha, I thought, now THIS is justice.
I liked the way the tables had turned . . . Blame the ten year old. What does a six year old know anyway?

Our parents deemed us equally responsible for the incident. The punishment for me was much milder than I anticipated. In fact, I think I was sent to my room for an hour. I didn't have to clean the go-go boot either. Not that Cathy would ever wear that boot again. The 60s were over, man.

* * *

Fortunately the trauma of this event didn't cause any lasting psychological damage for Cathy. Over time she took on more responsibility at The Poplars. By the mid 70s, she was an integral part of the staff. For a good part of my childhood, the summer months meant seeing Cathy infrequently as she was often busy doing something with someone. She was our babysitter for a short period of time when she was 12 or 13, but that was about it for our summer-time contact with Cathy.

Cathy started out as a chambermaid at the lodge when she was 14. She didn't take the job as seriously as some of the veteran chambermaids. The daily cleaning up after another person was a tedious task for her, so mischievous Cathy had to spice things up. She did this on many occasions as she became the official lodge prankster. What better way to carry out practical jokes than disguised as an innocent member of the housekeeping staff?

The guests knew Cathy as Pat and Joan's daughter. They teased her about finally having responsibility around the lodge and about having to clean their rooms. But Cathy could handle this teasing and began to target guests with her pranks. She was careful to choose only guests whom she felt could handle being the victim of a practical joke.

One of her favourites was short-sheeting the beds of unsuspecting guests. Many guests claimed the next morning that something was wrong with their sheets. They had pulled and pulled only to realize that someone had tampered with their sheets. My parents would shake their heads and feign ignorance knowing full well who was responsible.

Another of Cathy's favourite pranks involved putting Saran Wrap over the toilet bowl in guests' rooms. This joke was a lot nastier and messier. Only the most well-adjusted guests were targeted. And she only used it when it was necessary to make a statement about who was in charge at the lodge.

After one summer as a chambermaid, Cathy moved on to the dining room the next summer becoming a waitress at the age of 15. The opportunities for mischief in the dining room were few as most people don't take kindly to jokes involving their food. Cathy had to take her job more seriously. It represented a promotion for her.

The main concerns for any new waitress, especially a 15 year old, were remembering the guests' orders and holding on to a large tray piled high with full plates. For my parents, there was no sound more grating than the thunderous crash of a tray load hitting the dining-room floor. This was a regular occurrence for a rookie member of the wait staff. Cathy was no exception. In fact, she probably dropped more than her share of trays in her first summer.

When she wasn't working during the summer months, Cathy was busy with her friends, many of whom also worked at the lodge. During down times, Cathy and her bikini-clad friends would often take a boat out to swim at Hungry Bay, a secluded swimming hole where the water was clean and deep. Of course, I had my sights set on a few of her friends, but I decided to play it cool as usual to increase their desire for me. This plan never really worked, however.

* * *

My sister owned an impressive record collection, at least impressive by my standards. When she was away on one of her afternoon excursions, Steven, Paul and I would sneak into her bedroom to listen to her records.

She had albums from groups we had never heard of and music that was different from anything we had listened to. Her music trumped Dougie McViety's Simon and Garfunkel album. She had a 45 by the band Grand Funk Railroad. The song on this record was *Locomotion*, not the sappy 1960s version but a heavy distorted cover. This song was our introduction to hard rock. We put the song on repeat on her record player and danced like frantic cage dancers from the 1960s.

I think that she may have suspected something because this little 45 started to wear out by the end of that summer. She confronted us in the hallway outside her bedroom and demanded to know why her favourite 45 was so badly scratched. We ran away, confirming out guilt.

She also had albums by other bands too, including Led Zeppelin *IV* (we knew it as the album with the cover with the old guy carrying the pile of straw on his back), Nazareth's *Greatest Hits* (my introduction to the rock ballad tradition with *Love Hurts*), the Eagle's *Greatest Hits* (I loved *Witchy Woman*), and Alice Cooper's *Alice Cooper Goes to Hell.* Hell? We just had to listen to it. Plus the cover photo of Alice himself was frightening with his green face, blood shot eyes, and black lips. His lyrics for the title track were the first lyrics I committed to memory at the tender age of 11.

* * *

I have had few heroes in my life. Emotional investment in a hero is hard work, and heroes are not always up to the challenge. Cathy was my first hero and perhaps my only legitimate one. I worshipped her from a very young age. She was my big sister and my protector. Cathy's role in the firing of Helga, the wicked babysitter, was just the beginning of my adulation for her.

She was always cheerful. Her trademarks were her infectious, bright smile and her full body giggle. She kept my parents in line whenever they took the demands of the lodge and family life too seriously. The confrontations, check that, healthy debates between my sister and father were epic. The rest of us, including my mother the "old doll", would sit there awestruck by this precocious and opinionated teenager who challenged her "old man" on any number of issues. Throughout my childhood I wished I could be just like her.

Cathy, September 1979

* * *

A year and a half after we sold the lodge, Cathy and three of her friends were out driving on a country road one Friday night in late September. Cathy was in her final year of high school and was in the process of applying to university. We were living in Westport at the time, another small town, not far from Newboro.

The primary pastime for teenagers in small towns then (and today) was hanging out and going to house parties. Because friends would come from small towns all over the area, a vehicle was critical. On any Friday night there could be a house party in one town and a bush party ten miles away. Drinking and driving was all too common.

On their way to a party in Delta, my sister and her three friends spied another car pulled off to the side of County Rd. 42, just outside the village of Philipsville. Its four-way emergency lights were flashing. Cathy and her friends decided to stop and offer some help. They discovered that the car had struck a deer. The injured deer remained in the middle of the highway. The four of them, along with the occupants of the other car, pulled the deer to the side of the road. Then the four teenagers piled back into their car.

Cathy's close friend Kathy Maynard was driving. Rather than continuing on to the party in Delta, they decided to return to Westport. Kathy started to execute a three point turn across the highway. Just as they were in the middle of this turn their car either stalled or hesitated (no one knows for sure). At that moment a black Trans Am came screaming through Philipsville well in excess of the speed limit and struck them broadside. Three of them, including my sister, were killed instantly while the fourth victim died the next day in hospital.

The police investigation revealed that Howard Wright (of Delta), the driver of the Trans Am, was drunk and that his vehicle was traveling at a speed of 120 kilometres per hour in an 80 km/h zone when the accident occurred. The occupants of my sister's car had also been drinking that night, and Kathy Maynard's blood alcohol level had exceeded the legal limit. The Crown laid charges of dangerous driving and impaired driving against Wright, but for incomprehensible reasons—mainly a weak-kneed judge (James Newton) and a severely flawed judicial system—these charges didn't stick. He got off with a paltry $200 fine (50 bucks for each life he took) and nothing else. No driver's licence suspension, no admission of guilt, no apology to the families of his victims. Nothing.

In a harmonized universe, Howard Wright would have faced a lifetime of unbearable guilt because of his careless actions the early morning hours of September 29th, 1979. However, if Mr. Wright did experience any life-altering remorse it was short-lived as fewer than five months after he killed my sister and her friends, Brockville Police charged him with impaired driving and speeding once again, this time in Brockville.

In addition, he was charged with failing to appear in court following his February 16th arrest. His sentence this time around? Fourteen days in jail, three months probation and a condition that he "abstain from the consumption of alcohol". You be the judge.

As for my sister's death, we were devastated. But we chose to deal with the trauma in different ways. My mom got busy with her new nursing job in Brockville. My dad spent a lot of time on the road. My brother and I withdrew into ourselves and vanished. No one in our house talked about it for some time after the accident and even then only rarely.

People have on occasion asked me how long it takes to get over the death of a loved one. I have always considered this a callous question. It is a question that I am even to this day unable to answer, because more than 30 years later I have yet to "get over" the death of my sister Cathy.

The Skylight

The individual responsible for changing the name "Villa Dale" to The Poplars didn't have to look very far for inspiration. Two distinct species of poplar trees were well represented on the property. Tall and tapered Lombardy Poplars lined most of the property on the west running the length of the boundary fence right up to By Street. The more majestic Eastern Cottonwood Poplars, known by locals as Ontario Poplars, canopied the lawn in front of the main lodge near the waterfront. These well-established trees were close to 70 years old and almost 100 feet high. They towered over the buildings and other trees on the property. Next to the arched wooden bridge that connected the docks, these Eastern Cottonwoods were the property's most recognizable feature.

A mature Eastern Cottonwood's height and girth are comparable to any full-grown oak or maple tree. The problem with the Cottonwood, however, is that its branches are more brittle than other trees. On a windy day when most trees bend with the wind, an Eastern Cottonwood limb can snap, clear through. In a resort setting this natural part of the tree's life cycle is a serious problem, especially for unsuspecting guests.

My parents fretted about these namesake trees. They couldn't cut them down because they were the trademark of the lodge. They could attempt to trim them, but the trees had grown so tall that the higher branches were not accessible for the average pruning truck. Even if a suitable pruning truck were located, the vehicle would sink into the spongy soil that housed the septic tanks. It was an impossible situation. More than once, a heavy branch had snapped and nearly struck a guest. The only saving grace was that the snap of the branch was loud enough to startle the guest, causing him to look upward and to leap out of the way before the branch hit the ground.

This good fortune couldn't last forever. My parents knew this. First of all, they were concerned about someone, maybe even Paul or me, being hurt; and second, they were convinced that if someone were injured there would be a significant lawsuit. Paul and I had discussed the possibility of a lawsuit if we were ever struck by a falling tree branch.

Something had to be done. My dad decided to target specific branches that posed a greater threat than others. He just needed someone willing to do the work . . . cheaply. He concluded that he had to recruit someone with climbing and cutting abilities, preferably someone who had done this type of work before. He found a number of individuals willing to climb trees and chainsaw some troublesome branches. Of course, my dad chose to go with the tree cutter who submitted the lowest bid. The winner was a former Bell Canada employee too, so my dad was convinced he selected the right man for the job.

After extensive consultation between the tree-cutter and my father, they concluded the principal threat on the property was the over-grown Ontario Poplar that towered over the main lodge dining room. There was one branch in particular that was hanging precariously over the large antique glass skylight, the main lodge's most striking feature, which dated back to the 1920s. Many a starlit evening guests could enjoy a home cooked meal under the beauty of this one-of-a-kind window to the sky. The branch had to go.

The day came for the cutting and pruning. There was much anticipation on the grounds, with staff and guests alike curious to see this fearless lumberjack scale the tree solo, chainsaw and ropes in tow.

A crowd gathered on the lawn a safe distance from the cut; some dragged over lawn chairs for the show. Paul and I had prime seats in what turned out to be the front row. My anxious mother talked to some guests behind us. My aloof father stood off by himself, nervously pacing. It was early afternoon.

The tree cutter reached the designated point for his first and most significant cut. We watched his every move. He tied a rope around his waist and secured it to the main trunk. He was wearing telephone lineman's spiked boots, so there was no way he was going to fall from the tree. Slung over his shoulder was the rope he would tie first to the tree trunk and then around the branch to prevent it from plummeting to the ground. Everything seemed to be in place for a perfect cut. He appeared to know what he was doing. He started the chainsaw. We couldn't wait. This was going to be entertaining.

The chainsaw blade started into the brittle wood. At the halfway point in the cut, all was going as planned. He continued cutting and then voila he was clear through to the other side. He had completed the cut and the rope had held . . . for about five seconds. Then it gave way and the branch came crashing down . . . directly through the one-of-a-kind skylight.

Was this part of the plan? Paul and I wondered aloud.
The crowd on the lawn gasped and fell silent.
I heard my mother shout, *Oh my God!*

I looked at my dad. His face was ashen, his head down, eyes riveted to the ground. I looked back at the tree cutter. Chainsaw still running, he clung to the branch staring at the gaping hole in the roof of the dining room. I looked back in the direction of my father. He was gone. He must have gone into the lodge to inspect the damage I thought.

Curiosity got the best of everyone. My mother led a distraught group of guests and staff into the lodge and headed toward the dining room where she assumed she would find my dad and the horrible mess of the inch and a half thick shattered glass. My brother and I followed. When we arrived, we discovered the shattered glass, most of it deeply imbedded in the hardwood floor. The heavy poplar branch had destroyed the entire skylight. The thick green glass was strewn all over tables, chairs and floor. It was a disaster. Even after hours of cleanup and repair, the reminders of the skylight were clearly visible in the pock-marked wooden floor, tables and chairs.

Later that day, Louie covered the gaping hole in the roof with plywood, a temporary solution, until my parents could order a replacement skylight. Of course, my mother could not find my father as he disappeared immediately after the crash, only to return much later in the evening after my mom had sorted out the details of the accident and the subsequent repair. The magician had pulled his famous disappearing act once again, much to the chagrin of my mother who paid the tree cutter and informed him his services were no longer required.

After numerous phone calls to glass and window manufacturers all over Eastern Ontario, my parents gave up on their search for glass of the same quality, size and vintage. Louie's plywood repair job became permanent.

Tuesdays with Mom

Without my mother, the business of The Poplars would have been an abject failure. My dad was the face of the place or, as he used to remind us, the brains behind the operation. My mother was the heart of the lodge. She would wake very early every morning and in one of her cotton flowered print dresses, standard summer attire for the matron of a fishing resort in the 1970s, dash to the lodge kitchen. Even with a semi-reliable kitchen staff, my mother felt that only she could provide those special finishing touches to meals and service that kept the guests content and loyal. For the staff it was just a job. For my mother it was an opportunity to let her quiet and considerate personality shine through in everything she did.

On busy nights, Joan was frantic and in her element. She would assist and direct any staff member requiring help in the kitchen. She could be subtle or direct in her leadership, sometimes giving orders but more often leading by example—the "here, let me do it" school of leadership. She had little patience for incompetence in the kitchen or in the dining room.

One of her responsibilities was operating the large stainless steal meat slicer. Most evenings my mother was in the over-heated kitchen, glued to the electric slicer, cutting piece after piece of turkey, or ham, or roast beef.

It was supper time in early August. I was reclining on the grass in front of the main lodge, waiting for something exciting to transpire. In retrospect, I spent far too much time waiting for something to happen, still do. There were a few guests mulling about. The dining room was full. My dad was at the front desk. Bulbous clouds drifted overhead. The scene was idyllic.

A woman's scream shattered the calm. There was some commotion around the corner of the main lodge near the back entrance to the kitchen. I waited. My heart raced.

What disaster is it this time? I wondered.

I saw my mother tear up the hill in the direction of the parking lot. She was silent and appeared to be holding something in front of her. Close behind Ruth, the cook, hurried to keep up with my mom. My dad emerged from the screened in porch area. He observed Ruth chasing my mom. He sprinted in the direction of my mom and Ruth. He caught them at the edge of the parking lot.

I heard elevated voices. There was a heated exchange between Ruth and my dad with my dad pointing in the direction of the lodge kitchen. Ruth turned and headed back toward the kitchen entrance. My dad placed his arm around my mother's shoulder. Together they continued up the hill. I wouldn't see either until much later that evening.

I had no idea what happened. No one was around. No one noticed me alone on the lawn. No one knew I had witnessed the scene at the top of the hill.

I remained on the lawn. My imagination took hold. I pictured my mother. I pictured the meat slicer. I pictured flying fingers. I pictured blood everywhere. Decapitation. Culinary carnage.

My sister came out of the lodge, clad in her waitress attire. She had the task of rounding up her brothers. She explained to us what happened. Her explanation lacked detail; all she told us was that mom cut her finger and that she would be okay.

I don't recollect much else from that night except that Cathy was in charge. My brother and I waited anxiously for Mom to return. We refused to go to bed. Cathy refused to make us. She even let us watch a creepy episode of *Night Gallery*, Rod Serling's flawed but frightening attempt to recapture the magic of *The Twilight Zone*. The episode we watched involved an irrepressible vampire living in a crypt behind a stately country home. It didn't help our already delicate state of mind.

Close to midnight, lying in bed and still very much awake, we heard my mother and father at the front door. We flew down the stairs to find my mom and dad in the front hall. My sister greeted them and hugged my mother. Paul and I sat at the bottom of the stairs, not sure what to make of it all. My mother had an over-sized gauze bandage on her right hand. One finger stuck out prominently from the others.

She looked like she had been crying, her eyes were red, but she didn't seem that upset or in any pain either. Perhaps it was the painkillers, or more likely my father had taken her out for a few cocktails to ease the pain.

The next day over breakfast Paul and I heard the gruesome details. While trying to separate frozen hamburgers with a sharp knife, our mom told us, the knife slipped and sliced into the tip of her right index finger. It wasn't the menacing meat slicer after all. The knife went clear through the end of her finger and ruptured a blood vessel. Blood sprayed all over the kitchen and didn't stop spraying for sometime.

Someone, she couldn't remember who, wrapped a towel around her finger. She said she knew she had to get to the hospital right away, so she ran out the back door of the kitchen and headed up the hill to the car. She said it didn't occur to her who would drive. She thought maybe she would drive herself. That's when my dad and Ruth had had their short exchange. My dad helped my mom into the station wagon, and they headed to Kingston General Hospital.

My dad must have been in his element. The undercover police officer had a real emergency to deal with. I can picture the two of them racing down the back roads to Kingston. Perhaps my dad had his magnetic police light flashing on top of the station wagon. Perhaps he was busy on his CB radio making sure that all traffic up ahead was re-routed. Perhaps he arranged a police escort along the way. All of these things might have occurred. To this day, all my mother remembers is the speed at which my dad drove. They arrived in Kingston in record time.

At the hospital, there just happened to be a plastic surgeon on duty when my mother arrived. After the examination, he concluded that the knife had not only severed a blood vessel but also damaged a nerve. There was a strong possibility that my mom could lose the use of the top half of her middle finger. No more flipping the bird for her. But the surgeon was able to repair both the nerve and the blood vessel at the same time. He offered no guarantees with the nerve, but he was optimistic.

Within a year, my mother was able to use her middle finger just as she once had. Flipping the bird became a more frequent gesture, whenever guests asked her which finger she had injured the previous summer.

* * *

The middle child theory goes something like this or so I have been told: When the first child comes along his arrival is much-anticipated by his new parents. The build-up to the birth of this child is unmatched in its intensity for both parents. New parents read books, attend classes, alter diets, and sacrifice sleep—all for the sake of the well-being of this child.

The birth of this child is nothing short of a gift from God, with all parties involved, including first time grandparents, anointing the first born the Christ child. Every move, every sound, every gesture of this new human being is celebrated. First times and newness tend to do funny things to people, changing them from calm rational sorts to obnoxiously over-attentive doters. The first born has and will continue to have the undivided attention of his parents well into adulthood as he achieves milestone after milestone.

In a family with three children, the next birth of significance is the birth of the third child, the life-long baby of the family. This child represents the last kick at the can. He is the one who will benefit from the lessons learned from the previous two children. He will be forever babied, and for him the state of childhood will last longer than for the other two, perhaps well into adulthood. The rules, the expectations, the hierarchy will all be different for this youngest child. His relationships with siblings and parents will be tailored to his newness and his youth. Taken less seriously at times, treated less harshly at others, the youngest will struggle to make his mark and to establish himself as unique from his older siblings.

This brings me to the middle child, the one who is acknowledged and cared for like his siblings, but who doesn't have the associative baggage of the other two. This middle child flies under the radar because of the attention showered on the other two. The firsts of the first born are old by the time the second child achieves them. While his life is no less significant, the reactions to it are muted.

The middle child waddles through his early years stuck in a no-man's land. This child avoids attention for the wrong things and seeks attention for the right things but often receives neither. He has a front row seat for observing his siblings in all their glory, at times jealous but more often indifferent as this is the benign plight of the middle child.

* * *

My time as the youngest child lasted exactly 16 months, until the appearance of my brother in 1966. I was destined to be known as the middle child for the remainder of my childhood. Not that I minded. My parents would over-indulge us throughout the winter months, and there was not obvious favouritism. The summer months of neglect (as they saw them) were compensated for with grand holiday celebrations, quality time throughout the fall and winter months, and lengthy family vacations to Florida every March.

We did play the neglect card when necessary, often comparing our summers to the summers of some of our friends who did the more traditional summer things, like going to the beach, camping, having picnics, or escaping to the cottage. It was only later that we realized, of course, that the magic of our own summers far outweighed anything that our friends were up to during their summers. But we never let our parents in on the secret because guilt and over-indulgence work very well together, especially in a pseudo-Catholic household.

My sister Cathy was my mom's favourite, as she should have been. Her first born, Cathy was everything a first born should be: cute, angelic, low-maintenance, and seemingly innocent. Cathy didn't have a mean bone in her body. During her short time on the planet, she and my mom were inseparable, the strength of the bond between the two of them obvious. They were friends and confidantes.

For me it was my relationship with my dad that mattered most to me, or at least that made itself matter most. As it turned out, we had a lot in common. We had similar temperaments, and this brought us together. He and I were as close as a father and son could be.

Paul and my dad had an acrimonious relationship from the beginning, perhaps hampered by Paul's sleeping difficulties that manifested themselves very early on in life. Paul's antics in the first couple years of life prompted my dad to often seek solace at a nearby motel in suburban Montreal. They didn't get off to the best of starts. My brother's fondness for things strange really didn't mesh with my dad's idea of meaningful and interesting pursuits. Early on in their relationship it was evident that they just didn't understand each other.

To compensate for this 'neglect' on the part of my father, my mother babied Paul. Enabled might be a better word. She may deny this, but Paul was her baby; and the treatment he received from her (just like the treatment I received from my father) was preferential to say the least. I think Paul deserved this; someone had to give him attention. My mom was this someone.

My relationship with my mother appeared to be secondary when compared to her relationships with my brother and sister. But because I had my dad's undivided attention, this lack of a relationship with my mother never bothered me on a conscious level; God knows what was going on on a subconscious level.

* * *

Out of this dynamic, however, developed one of the more meaningful traditions of my childhood: the time I spent with my mother in the lodge kitchen every Tuesday in the summer months.

Tuesday was officially my mother's day as The Poplars' cook. She did an admirable job producing pre-packed cookout lunches, breakfast for up to 70 guests, lunch for fewer guests and dinner for the same 70 as breakfast. The harried pace in the kitchen and in the dining room did not allow for much downtime or reflection. The food was tasty and wholesome but not fancy.

Between breakfast and lunch on Tuesdays, my mother was often alone in the kitchen, and for two hours she would have time to plan the dinner menu, order supplies or experiment with a new culinary creation. The peaceful atmosphere in the kitchen at these times was in stark contrast to the frenzied pace of earlier or later in the day. I am not certain if I was invited or if I just happened to show up one day, but I soon realized that Tuesday mornings in the kitchen I had her undivided attention; and she had mine.

She was different during this time. She seemed interested in what I had been up to or what I was going to be up to. It wasn't that she wasn't interested in these things before; it's just that we, I mean she, never had the time to talk about the more mundane activities of a child—not just any child, her lovechild with the milkman in Montreal of course—during the summer months. Little did she know that most of these activities weren't dull at all . . . but that is what I led her to believe.

The tradition was simple as it evolved. I discovered I wanted to spend my Tuesday mornings with my mother helping her in the kitchen. That was the incentive for me. There was no ulterior motive. The helping morphed into a weekly tradition of making a large batch of oatmeal chocolate chip cookies, a family recipe that had been passed down to her and one that she used on special occasions. I think she understood that Tuesdays constituted a special occasion.

The two of us—I the helper, she the baker—made chocolate chip cookies. Much of the cookie dough didn't survive to become fully baked cookies. In fact, I didn't care if one cookie was ever produced as it was the dough that was the best part. My mom didn't seem to care either although the batch was so large that some baked cookies were inevitable.

The conversation was secondary to the fact that I was just hanging out with my mom. Closer to lunch a more professional air would take over the kitchen, as staff arrived for the lunch-time rush. Even then my mom seemed oblivious to the demands of others. While the lunch menu was predetermined, my mother was always willing to alter the menu and make something special for me.

"What would you like for lunch today, Jimmy?" she would inquire, knowing the answer. It was the same answer every week.

Playing along, I would ask, "Mom, can I have grilled cheese and French fries please?"
"But, Jimmy, you had that last week, didn't you?" she would reply.
'I don't remember," I would say. "But it's my favourite, you know."
"Of course," she conceded. "How could I forget?"

I would end our Tuesdays together eating my favourite lunch while sitting at the staff lunch table across from the main cooking area. From my vantage point, I would marvel at my mom's calm, professional manner as she slipped back into head cook mode and faced the onslaught of the lunch-time rush.

Mary

Mary was a girl who taught me all I had to know.
She put me right on my first mistake. Summer wasn't
gone when I learnt all she had to show. Really gave
all a boy could take.

—Chilliwack ("Arms of Mary",
Down from the Valley, 1978)

One of my major regrets about my parents' decision to sell the lodge is that they decided to sell just before I became a teenager. I was 12 years old in the summer of 1977 and just starting to appreciate the opposite sex on a more regular basis, make that a nightly basis. Daytime too. The Poplars would have been a perfect place to spend my teenage years and offered numerous opportunities to meet some like-minded teenage girls, also known as fishermen's daughters.

It wasn't that I didn't have any experience with girls. I was the first boy in my grade one class to kiss a girl. I remember it like it was the day before yesterday, assuming of course I had been in a coma for 40 years. Her name was Charalee Rice, and she was the prettiest girl in all of grade one at Rideau Vista Public School in Westport. I was infatuated with her. She used to wear the shortest pink dresses. She had a beautiful smile and was the smartest in our class. I used to think about her all the time and tried to sit beside her in class and be near her at recess.

One day in a moment of unprecedented courage I decided to make my move. We were sitting alone together on the steps at the side entrance to the school. It was lunch hour recess. We talked, flirted is the more appropriate term. Completely unsolicited I leaned over and gave Charalee a kiss on the cheek. Her face turned red, and mine turned even redder. She didn't recoil or protest. Then the bell rang. That was the extent of our relationship: one stolen kiss on the steps of Rideau Vista Public School when I was in grade one.

Every year I thought, *Okay now is the time I reveal my deep love for Charalee.* But every year I chickened out, giving up altogether by the time I was in grade eight. What ever happened to the confident Jimmy of grade one is a mystery for the ages.

After my stolen kiss, it's fair to say I had a few dry years. Sure there were the babysitters, but that was one-way love; and I was all talk and zero action with them.

All that appeared about to change in the summer of 1977.

Mary Sable was a year older than I. She was from Bethlehem, Pennsylvania. Mary from Bethlehem. Imagine the role playing possibilities later on in life with this one. She was staying at the lodge with her parents and her older cousin, an overtly sexual 15 year old. Her older cousin spent most of her time conducting an aggressive teenage manhunt around the lodge and had taken to romancing one of the busboys at the lodge, an inevitable outcome to say the least.

Mary didn't like to fish. Consequently, The Poplars didn't have much to offer an adolescent teenage girl with a burgeoning sexuality. Abandoned by her parents and by her promiscuous cousin, Mary was on her own most of the time.

Perfect.

Mary was at least five inches taller than I was. She had shoulder length curly dark brown hair and a darker complexion. I think she was part Italian and part Irish. She was slim and had braces on her teeth. Thankfully, like many teenage girls in the 1970s, Mary wore snug fitting Levis and tank tops most of the time. In the evening when it was cooler she wore a white cable knit sweater. Oh yeah, and she had something else too . . . breasts. They were just developing, but make no mistake—they were breasts.

Breasts.
Two of them.

In 1977 braces adorned my teeth, and this may have brought us together that summer at The Poplars. While I spent my free-time (I had no other type of time when I was twelve) playing around the lodge, we had replaced cowboys and Indians with pick-up sports, mainly touch football, which we played on the main lawn of the lodge. I was able to throw the football farther and more accurately than most of my friends. I couldn't run very well, so I often played quarterback.

Being the quarterback and also the resort owners' son may have worked in my favour with Mary too. Perhaps she wasn't that shallow. Maybe it was just me after all. Because Mary didn't have much to keep her occupied during the day, she was a frequent spectator for these contests.

This is when I began to notice her. She may have participated in a game or two, but I don't recall. I remember that she possessed a shy but pretty smile and that she used to keep her mouth closed when she smiled. I was familiar with this strategy as it was one I employed as well.

It took a least a couple more touch football games before I decided that she was someone who I wanted to get to know.

At the conclusion of one of our games, when Mary was sitting on the picnic table on the sidelines, I sat down beside her. The exact words of the conversation that afternoon elude me, but it may have had something to do with our shared experiences with braces or perhaps the on-going tensions in the Middle East. Soon I discovered that talking to Mary was easy. She was shy. I was shy. But around Mary my shyness disappeared.

She seemed interested in me as well, which is perhaps one of the best cures for shyness there is. I was definitely interested in her. She was exquisite, especially her enchanting brown eyes. Her soft, gentle voice was easy to listen to. And she looked fantastic in her Levis.

Breasts.

After our meeting on the picnic table, we spent the remainder of her stay with each other. We were together every day for a week. I soon lost interest in the infantile games of Paul and my friends. All I wanted to do was be with Mary. She seemed to feel the same way too. We would play pool, sit on the dock, go for walks; we even held hands once, but only briefly. I liked the fact that I was different around her—more confident, funnier, and relaxed.

It was all because of Mary and her gentle, warm breasts, I mean personality.

But Mary's stay wasn't going to last forever. We both knew that. I recall feeling upset about this reality but not as upset as I should have been. We were confident we would see each other the following summer, and we would carry on where we left off.

On Mary's last night at The Poplars, we sat alone together on the veranda outside her room. The sky was dark. The crickets were chirping. The fireflies glowing. The night was quiet with most guests having retired for the evening. It was just Mary and me.

Now was my chance. Perhaps that second kiss that had eluded me since grade one would happen. Charalee Rice was a distant memory. We were sitting close enough on the creaky wooden loveseat that our shoulders and legs were touching. It was a cool night, so Mary was wearing her white sweater. If I were a betting man I would say that a kiss was only minutes away as we sat, talked, and looked into each other's eyes. She was beautiful. I was confident. Finally, my moment had arrived.

Then out of the heavens came a voice. It was an intrusive, loud voice. A voice so penetrating and perplexing that it made me shudder. It was my mother's voice. She was on the intercom, volume cranked high.

My dad being the paranoid, surveillance freak that he was had installed two-way intercom speakers in strategic locations all over the property earlier in the decade. These speakers were in trees, they were on rooftops, they were on flag poles, they were even in bird houses. At any point during the day, my dad could listen in on conversations all over the lodge property. This was one of his favourite pastimes. These speakers were two-way, so anyone could speak to my dad too if he revealed his presence and spoke first. The command centre for this elaborate system was his off-limits office in our house.

To this day, I remember my mother's piercing voice and her unfortunate choice of words on the intercom that fateful night: "JIMMY, IT'S TIME FOR BED. COME UP TO THE HOUSE RIGHT AWAY."

I was humiliated. "Jimmy, it's time for bed"? Come on! Couldn't she at least come up with some sort of secret code like, "Agent 029, please report to headquarters immediately"? How difficult would that have been? Heck, a code name would have only enhanced my allure with the ladies.

The timing couldn't have been worse. The kiss was moments away, but my mother and more specifically my father and his 1970's Richard Nixon-induced paranoia ruined what was going to be the pivotal moment of my life up to that point.

"But, Mom," I pleaded. "Can't I stay up just a little bit longer?"
"No, Jimmy," she replied. "It's already past your bedtime."
"Mom, please!" I begged.
"Sorry, Jimmy, not tonight."

Not tonight? Did she have any idea what "tonight" meant to me? Not tonight? How could she be so insensitive to me and my needs as a soon to be teenage boy? And besides, real lovers don't have bedtimes.

Our Romeo and Juliet moment was lost. Mary and I resigned ourselves to the fact that the kiss wasn't going to happen that night. But we were both hopeful despite the setback. We would spend her entire visit together next summer we reassured each other. I bid her good night. In the bitter darkness, I made my way up the hill to the house.

The next morning I would be there for Mary's departure. But it wasn't the same. Her parents and her cousin were present. There was no time for a meaningful exchange between the two of us. It was just a simple goodbye, a wave and "I'll see you next summer."

Our summer love affair was over.

It was our intention to write to each other over the fall and winter months. We did this for a while, but I was not much of a letter writer. Her letters were long and eloquent. She acknowledged how much she missed me. I tried to sound romantic in my few letters to her, but I couldn't pull it off. I even enlisted my sister's help on one of the letters because she was the only person in whom I could confide about my feelings for Mary. The letters didn't sound like me, nor did they come close to capturing the essence of my longing for her.

My letters to Mary ceased, and my focus shifted to next summer and our inevitable reunion. Mary's letters kept coming, however, and her interest and warmth were as genuine as they had ever been. She was committed to keeping in touch over the long term, and her frequent letters revealed the depths of her commitment to me. I was not worthy.

In the early months of 1978 my parents made a hasty and shocking decision. They were going to put The Poplars up for sale and try to have a new owner in place for the beginning of April. This was no April Fool's joke either. Something to do with the bottom line, the over-heated Canadian dollar, the overhead of the operation, brittle tree branches, drunken midgets . . . who knows for sure.

I never saw Mary again.

Burning the Leaves

After Labour Day the pace of life at the lodge slowed. School arrived abruptly every September. It was the finality of it all that struck me. One minute I had unlimited independence and opportunity for adventure; the next I was sitting under harmful fluorescent lighting on a hard metal seat in a musty elementary school classroom. It didn't seem fair at all, but there was nothing I could do about it so the unhappiness subsided, usually by the first recess. But the lodge was still the lodge on weekends in September and October.

The activities around The Poplars were different in the fall. While it was fully operational right up until the day after the Canadian Thanksgiving, the busyness of the place was reserved for the summer months. Weekends throughout the fall, hardcore fishermen would arrive for one last shot at fishing immortality, trying to catch that record sized bass or pike and maybe win a Hudson Bay blanket or coat. From a kid's perspective the prizes were lame. Perhaps a boat and motor combination would have been a greater incentive. Why wasn't I put in charge of the marketing campaigns at The Poplars? We would have been in the poorhouse in no time. But wait . . . we were in the poorhouse . . . that's why we sold the place—apparently.

As the temperature decreased in the fall, the warmth of the main lodge increased. This was due in part to roaring fire that my father kept burning until closing day in October. In the mornings as Paul, Cathy and I marched down to the lodge kitchen for breakfast before heading off to catch the school bus, we could see wisps of smoke rising from the lodge chimney. The brisk autumn air and the sweetness of the maple smoke produced an invigorating combination.

During the week when we were at school, I had no idea what went on at the lodge. There were some guests who preferred the solitude of the autumn season, but there were fewer demands on my parents in the fall. My dad had even more time for golf. I am not sure if this slow season also meant more time for my parents to spend with each other. The hectic pace of the summer months dictated that their time together was brief; perhaps in the fall they made up for this by going for walks, having lunch together or sitting by the lake.

Rare photo featuring my parents together at the lodge

September was over before we knew it, and Thanksgiving arrived. Thanksgiving weekend was one last opportunity for celebrations and goodbyes before The Poplars closed for winter. Guests, some making their second or third visits of the season, arrived on the Friday and stayed through until Monday. Even though they weren't Canadian and had no reason to celebrate our Thanksgiving holiday, they realized that this was their last opportunity to experience the rustic comforts of The Poplars. The visitors who stayed until the end were the ones who had been coming to the lodge for years. They knew the place and the lake as well as we did. They felt that it was their home, so it was only fitting that they be there until the end.

Thanksgiving weekend culminated in one final celebratory shore dinner on one of the provincial islands on Newboro Lake. This cookout combined thank yous and farewells all at once, with select staff and specially invited guests present. The best part for Paul and me was that it meant one last excursion in a boat, and one last opportunity for exploration. Three or four cedar strip boats with 9.9 horsepower Evinrude outboard motors set out from the lodge at noon and arrived at a designated island for the season-ending celebration.

Louie was there, my mom and dad, fishing guides Art Pritchard and Tommy Pritchard too, and any other staff members who happened to be available. So, too, were the specially invited guests who knew they were part of the inner circle of The Poplars. Most of the participants in the cookout wore thick flannel jackets, particularly the red and black checkered kind. The autumn air was cool, and the transformation of the leaves from green to shades of crimson, orange and yellow was well underway. Mirroring the cobalt sky and the vibrant fall colours, the lake was at its most scenic in the fall.

Apart from our exploration of the remote island, the food was the highlight for Paul and me. The aromas and the tastes were exquisite. The fare was traditional Newboro Lake shore dinner: pan fried bass, boiled potatoes, smoked oysters and . . . wait for it . . . bacon turned golden brown in a pound of lard. All prepared over an open fire. The smoke was everywhere: in our hair, in our clothes, and in our eyes. But we weren't bothered by it. Coffee made from lake water was also on the menu, but that was an acquired taste that eluded me. It was a delectable feast, apart from the obvious lack of roughage. Of course, there was copious booze, too. The late afternoon banquet was the same every year, and every year just as enjoyable.

* * *

After the Thanksgiving long weekend all that remained for us to do at the lodge was to prepare the buildings and property for winter. My dad did a final tally of the season's losses, but this was a solitary affair between him and the ledger sheet. Housekeeping staff scrubbed guest rooms from floor to ceiling. Louie, his son Bruce, and my father boarded up windows, turned off water and electricity supplies, and hauled boats out of the lake. Moth balls were the seasonal scent of the time with each guest room receiving its annual dose. What do moth balls do anyway? Are moths really a problem in the dead of winter in a frigid and boarded-up building? The preventative moth balls were everywhere. It never occurred to me to ask for an explanation.

By mid October, poplar and maple leaves covered the grounds of The Poplars. Because the volume of leaves was so great, the options for disposal were limited. We could spend days raking, bagging and carting leaves to the dump where they would be burned, or we could skip the middle man and do the burning right on site. There were no guests around so small fires all over the grounds were not bad for business. There were no environmental police back then either.

Every October my dad rounded up as many workers as he could find to spend weekends raking, piling and burning leaves. Paul and I and our friends were included in this year-end tradition early on in our lives. For the first time we felt we were contributing to the family business in a meaningful way.

Our idea of hard work and raking leaves was different from my father's, however. His concept was simple: rake the leaves into piles, take very few breaks and then burn the piles. Of course the whole point of raking leaves when one is a kid is to build the highest possible mountain of leaves, which we then converted into complex leaf forts with outer ramparts, gun turrets, estate rooms, antechambers and secret passageways. Our leaf forts were elaborate works of art that took hours to create. Steven Moore would be there, Greg Childs and Dougie McViety, too, and we recruited countless others to get the job done.

When we weren't building leaf fortresses, we were jumping from the pickup truck tailgate onto the soft mounds of leaves. While fire had its appeal, we dreaded my father lighting the match because it signalled the destruction of our castles. But before we knew it, the rapidly combusting leaves and their pleasing scent had us mesmerized. Any anguish over the loss of yet another leaf fortress vanished.

There were pockets of fire all over the grounds of The Poplars but especially on the lawn by the waterfront; and the glowing embers and the billowing smoke, late in the afternoon with the lake as a backdrop, created an other-world quality. The place looked like a war zone, I suppose. For us kids it appeared more like the smouldering remnants of a fire-happy Wizard of Id looking to wreak havoc one last time before the snows of winter hit.

Appendices

Annual Newsletter—drawn by Westport artist Jim Janeway

OUR 1977 SPRING NEWSLETTER — The Poplars

WE ARE PROUD TO BE STARTING OUR 10TH YEAR AT THE LODGE AND GRATEFUL TO ALL OUR FRIENDS WHO HAVE VISITED US THESE PAST YEARS. WE PLEDGE TO CONTINUE IMPROVING OUR SERVICES AND HOSPITALITY, TO ENSURE YOU ENJOYABLE SUMMER VACATIONS.

WINTER AT THE POPLARS HAS BEEN THE OLD FASHIONED TYPE BEGINNING WITH A VERY COLD DECEMBER. ICE IN THE LAKE HAS REACHED THREE FEET THICK.

THE TALLONS AND NEIGHBOURS HAVE KEPT ACTIVE WITH CROSS COUNTRY SKIING, JOGGING AND SKATING ON A HOME MADE RINK ON THE POPLARS PARKING LOT. ONE HOCKEY GAME PROVED UNFORTUNATE FOR PAT WHEN HIS WRIST WAS BROKEN BY A CRUEL BODY CHECK FROM LITTLE DAUGHTER CATHY.

THE POPLARS OPENS WITH PIKE SEASON ON SATURDAY MAY 14TH. BASS SEASON OPENS ON SATURDAY JUNE 25TH WHICH IS THE SAME DAY AS PAT'S BIRTHDAY. REGARDLESS OF WHAT HE SAYS THIS IS SHEER COINCIDENCE.

AS ALWAYS FISHING LICENCES CAN BE PURCHASED RIGHT AT THE LODGE. TO AVOID DISAPPOINTMENT BE SURE TO RESERVE YOUR FAVORITE ROOM AND GUIDE AT AN EARLY DATE. MANY WILL BE HAPPY TO HEAR WARD HALL HAS BEEN RENOVATED.

OUR "POPLARS GIANT" FISHING CONTEST WINNERS OF 1976 ARE JUDGE E. GANGLOFF OF SCHUYLKILL HAVEN PENN. (5 lb. 6 oz. LARGE MOUTH BASS.) — DAVE GREER OF BEACH HAVEN, NEW JERSEY (4 lb. 12 oz. SMALL MOUTH BASS). — A. JEFF GUIFFRE OF WATERBURY CONN. (8 lb. 12 oz. WALLEYE) — BARRY MEYERS OF READING, PENN (7 lbs. 12 oz. NORTHERN PIKE. THESE TALENTED FISHERMEN ALL RECEIVE HUDSON BAY BLANKETS AND PRO FISH'ENCY DIPLOMAS.

THIS SEASON THE POPLARS WILL TRY GUIDED BOAT TOURS OF THE BEAUTIFUL SURROUNDING LAKES.

WE LOOK FORWARD TO YOUR VISIT THIS SUMMER AND THE EVENING SNACKS AROUND THE OLD COFFEE POT.

SEE YOU FOR OUR 10TH ANNIVERSARY!

PAT & JOAN TALLON

BARNABY — PAUL — SKIPPER — JIMMY — MARSHMALLOW

TELEPHONE 613-272-2345 ANYTIME THROUGHOUT THE YEAR.

1977 Newsletter—artist Jim Janeway

A Johnny Hart cartoon: Art imitating life?

Even family pet Skipper got in on the act

Daughter Harper's original *Running the Sheets* cover concept (August 2006, age 10)

Acknowledgments

There are many people I need to thank for their direct or indirect involvement with this project.

Without the regular encouragement of my two kids, Harper and Patrick, I would have forgotten the details of these stories long ago. Thank you both for reminding me of the value of stories.

My spouse Nicole's resolute confidence in my writing ability and her regular reminders to put pen to paper were invaluable.

Thanks to Rick and Joan White, current proprietors of The Poplars, for their conscientious stewardship and for keeping the dinner bell alive and well.

I am indebted to muse/critic Jessica Tester. Your honest and enthusiastic feedback and encouragement throughout the writing process were invaluable.

Thanks to Barbara Bell for agreeing to read this book in its early stages and for her thoughtful commentary on both form and content.

I would like to acknowledge the fine work of Jenna at Staples who brought some old photographs back to life for this book.

I am also grateful to the village of Newboro and its remarkable inhabitants both past and present and to cartoonist Johnny Hart and his fellow travelers from south of the border.

My esteemed colleague and renowned grammarian Jackie RushMorgan provided some very helpful last minute proofreading as well as some astute editing suggestions.

Thanks to Richard Dunn and everyone at Xlibris Publishing for providing aspiring writers with publishing options that are exciting, comprehensive and professional.

Finally, thanks to my extraordinary parents for their willingness to not play it safe and for providing their children with some incredible memories.

Edwards Brothers Malloy
Thorofare, NJ USA
April 29, 2013